BROTHER & ME

Thomas Jackson & the Underground Railroad . . .
Westbury & Jericho many generations ago

A H I S T O R I C A L   N O V E L

M.W. 1850

THE RUNAWAY
SLAVE CAME TO MY
PLACE HE STOPT
OUTSIDE.
HE STAYED WITH
ME A WEEK BEFORE
HE RECUPERATED
AND PASS'D NORTH

BROTHER & ME

Thomas Jackson & the Underground Railroad . . .
Westbury & Jericho many generations ago

A H I S T O R I C A L N O V E L

Kathleen G. Velsor, Ed.D.

Acknowledgements

I am sincerely grateful to the reviewers of my manuscript—among them Long Island historians Gene Alexander Peters, James Driscoll, and Robert Hughes—for their meticulous attention to details, helping me confirm and clarify the actual facts from which this fictional account is drawn.

I am grateful for the respect and support given to me by my editor and publisher and friend, Terry Walton. It is only through her kind vision and deep caring for Anna and Brother that this story can be told.

Many thanks to my colleague Sara Blackburn, who insisted that I write this story as historical fiction. Thanks to Inger Gibb for her creativity and keen sense of design that has helped the characters to jump off the pages and into the minds of young readers. Thanks to photographer Michael Fairchild of Photosynthesis, who helped to bring our family together. Special thanks as well to Charla Bolton, Richard Klein, and Elizabeth Powers for varied kinds of assistance!

Thanks to the many research librarians who assisted me in the gathering of much-needed material: Norine Baskin, SUNY Old Westbury, Gwen Erickson, Guilford College Library, Greensboro, North Carolina, Betsey Murphy, Jericho Public Library, Jeanie Renison, Westbury Public Library, and historian Lynda Day, who encouraged me to research the Underground Railroad. And very special thanks to the staff at the Queens Historical Society and to local historian Richard Gachot, for the use of images from their collections.

To my students at Old Westbury, my heartfelt thanks—for all of their words of encouragement through the many stages of this manuscript, and for their genuine excitement about this work of historical fiction based in fact.

And certainly to my husband Curtis, who said "This is a great story!"

© 2005 Kathleen G. Velsor
Rosalie Ink Publications ▪ PO Box 291 ▪ Cold Spring Harbor, NY 11724 ▪ RosalieInk.com
First Edition ▪ All rights reserved
Editing & Production by Terry Walton ▪ Design by Inger Gibb
Printed by Avon Press, Hauppauge, NY
Library of Congress Control Number: 2005932720 ▪ ISBN 0-9711869-3-6

"Make no small plans—they have no power to move men's hearts."
- *As recalled by the late Leon Rushmore, of the Westbury Quakers'*
quiet and vital role in the Underground Railroad

"Students must know history in all of its complexities,
including its legacies of prejudice and discrimination, resilience and courage."
- *Underground Railroad Teaching Partnership*

Dedication

In loving memory of Jean Renison, Curator of the Historical Society
of the Westburys Collection at the Westbury Public Library, and of Leon A. Rushmore
of Westbury Meeting—and in celebration of all the stories we shared.

VELSOR

"Incidentally, Anna, linen is a very important commodity to the families who lived in Jericho. It's made from flax. Do you know what that is?"

Contents

Timeline – Thomas Jackson's Story

1643* John Jackson comes to Long Island from New England, settles in township of Hempstead

1687* John Jackson (son of John Jackson) petitions for 200 acres of land for sawmill on Jerusalem River, in present-day Wantagh

1702* First of three Westbury Meeting Houses is built on current site

1754 Brother's forebear Thomas Jackson is born into slavery, New York City

1763 Thomas Jackson's master Isaac Jackson dies in New York City and Thomas goes to Mr. M_____ and to Jackson Mill for help

1770 Thomas leaves Jackson Mill and goes to Seaman house in Jericho

1771* Elias Hicks marries Jemima Seaman from Jericho

1775* Elias Hicks meets with Society of Friends in Westbury and asks members to free their slaves

1785 Thomas Jackson meets Sallie at Willis Farm; they are soon married

1787* Jericho Meeting House is built on today's Old Jericho Turnpike

1804* Valentine Hicks marries Elias Hicks's daughter Abigail

1826-28* Young Henry Highland Garnet attends African Free School in New York City, and afterwards ships out to see the world

1829* Henry Highland Garnet comes to Willis home in Locust Grove (near Jericho); then to Epenetus Smith's house in Smithtown

1838* Frederick Douglass escapes to freedom

1844 Thomas Jackson writes his memoir; dies later that year at age 90

1850 M.W. cross-stitches sampler verse

• • •

1955 Anna Willis visits Brother and writes Notebooks 1 and 2

* Indicates historical fact

Prologue, "In My Imaginings . . ."

"Out of this suitcase came the imaginary account
of Anna Willis and her friend Brother, and of the notebooks and papers
that record their discoveries."

In 1985 my husband and I purchased a turn-of-the-century summer home in Bayville, Long Island, from a local businessman. He had bought the home with aspirations of using the property for commercial use. The Village denied his application, however, and we soon became the proud owners of our home overlooking Mill Neck Creek.

Recently, we decided to renovate the attic for work and studio space. While we were cleaning out the attic I discovered a small suitcase hidden behind some of our unopened moving boxes. The suitcase is scuffed brown leather and from its intriguing contents appears to be very old. Out of this suitcase came the imaginary account of Anna Willis and her friend Brother, and of the notebooks and papers that record their discoveries. Anna, Brother, and Thomas Jackson's life and memoir exist only in my mind and heart, yet their story is drawn from actual historical documents of the day.

Why did I choose "historical novel" for the story of the Underground Railroad in Westbury and Jericho? It was my wish to gather fascinating true facts for the most diverse audience possible – for fourth graders in their local history curriculum . . . for the inquiring minds of young adults . . . for high school and college students eager to make their own discoveries and conduct further research. And, I personally found the historical novel the most pleasing and effective way to convey this important story.

The Timeline (page 2) and Author's Note (page 89) confirm what is fact and what is historical fiction. Yet this is an intricate story – which people and which buildings were actual participants in the Underground Railroad? What is unproven rumor and what can be confirmed as truth? Further, the story has its own natural confusions. Everybody seems to have the same names (slaves often took their master's last name at emancipation; cousins married distant cousins in the custom of the day). Buildings were built in different parts with differing ages. Reliable sources sometimes conflict in names, dates, and other details. Records were scarce because helping fugitive slaves was a compassionate act that could land the helper in prison. Legends abound.

My aim as researcher and author? To challenge a whole new generation of students to think, to talk, to explore, to work with their teachers, to join me in the search for the full true story of the Underground Railroad in Westbury and Jericho . . . and perhaps in other Long Island towns as well.

★ ★ ★

. . . In my imaginings the contents of our old brown suitcase seemed at first to be just a collection of a prior owner's family history papers. I found an old newspaper clipping, some photographs, and a map showing part of the town of Oyster Bay and North Hempstead. There's also a folded piece of brown paper with the memoir of someone named Thomas Jackson, dated 1844. It was larger than our usual paper today, folded carefully into six parts as if to fit into a pocket, or an envelope. I also found lists of family names and their relatives dating back to before the Revolutionary War. There's even a copy of a 1941 speech made by the well-known local Quaker Henry Hicks for the 77th anniversary of freeing slaves in Westbury, and various other odd bits of information about Old Jericho.

My husband and I were fascinated by the contents, but none of the information made much sense to us until we came across two small slightly tattered old composition books tucked into the silk pocket of the suitcase. Each book was labeled "Brother and Me, by Anna Willis." They were numbered Notebook 1 and Notebook 2.

The little books are written like journals, with the dates of young Anna Willis's meetings with her down-the-street friend Brother. She recorded her own thoughts, as well as her word-by-word conversations with Brother.

Brother's words were intriguing for sure. He told Anna the story of a young slave from New York City who escaped from being sold when his master died in 1763. His escape was made possible through the kindness of Quaker families on Long Island. This information shines new light on the "freedom trail" through Long Island—the secret pathway to freedom that is only now being fully revealed—which helped set the stage for the later national abolitionist efforts to free enslaved individuals through an extraordinary series of connections that Americans now call the Underground Railroad.

We haven't yet found any records of Anna Willis herself, but are still searching. Perhaps her two notebooks were left behind on purpose, so that their discoverers could share Anna's story with other school-age children who seek to understand the meaning of freedom. KV

Illustrations

All listed images are from historical archives and local collections.

The Hicks-Seaman Family Tree

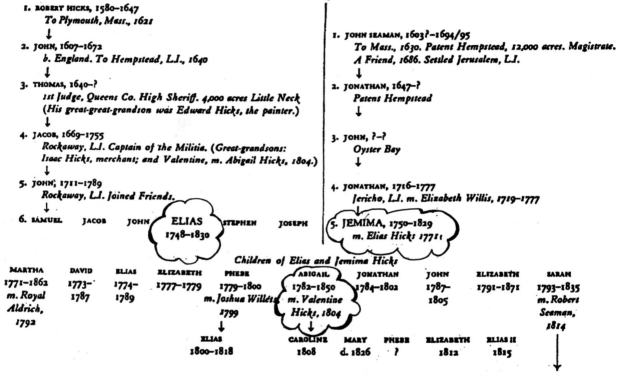

1. **ROBERT HICKS**, 1580–1647
   To Plymouth, Mass., 1621
   ↓
2. **JOHN**, 1607–1672
   b. England. To Hempstead, L.I., 1640
   ↓
3. **THOMAS**, 1640–?
   *1st Judge, Queens Co. High Sheriff. 4,000 acres Little Neck
   (His great-great-grandson was Edward Hicks, the painter.)*
   ↓
4. **JACOB**, 1669–1755
   *Rockaway, L.I. Captain of the Militia. (Great-grandsons:
   Isaac Hicks, merchant; and Valentine, m. Abigail Hicks, 1804.)*
   ↓
5. **JOHN**, 1711–1789
   Rockaway, L.I. Joined Friends.
   ↓

1. **JOHN SEAMAN**, 1603?–1694/95
   *To Mass., 1630. Patent Hempstead, 12,000 acres. Magistrate.
   A Friend, 1686. Settled Jerusalem, L.I.*
   ↓
2. **JONATHAN**, 1647–?
   Patent Hempstead
   ↓
3. **JOHN**, ?–?
   Oyster Bay
   ↓
4. **JONATHAN**, 1716–1777
   Jericho, L.I. m. Elizabeth Willis, 1719–1777
   ↓

6. **SAMUEL**   **JACOB**   **JOHN**   **ELIAS 1748–1830**   **STEPHEN**   **JOSEPH**   5. **JEMIMA**, 1750–1829 *m. Elias Hicks 1771*

Children of Elias and Jemima Hicks

| MARTHA 1771–1862 m. Royal Aldrich, 1792 | DAVID 1773–1787 | ELIAS 1774–1789 | ELIZABETH 1777–1779 | PHEBE 1779–1800 m. Joshua Willets 1799 | ABIGAIL 1782–1850 m. Valentine Hicks, 1804 | JONATHAN 1782–1802 | JOHN 1787–1805 | ELIZABETH 1791–1871 | SARAH 1793–1835 m. Robert Seaman, 1814 |

↓ (under PHEBE): **ELIAS 1800–1818**

↓ (under ABIGAIL): **CAROLINE 1808**   **MARY d. 1826**   **PHEBE ?**   **ELIZABETH 1812**   **ELIAS II 1815**

↓ (under SARAH):

**PHEBE ?; HANNAH, 1817; WILLET, 1818; ELIZABETH, 1820;
ELIAS, 1826; MARY, 1828; WILLET H., 1822**

- *From Elias Hicks, Quaker Liberal
(Columbia University Press 1956)
b= born, m= married, d= died*

The Willis Family Tree

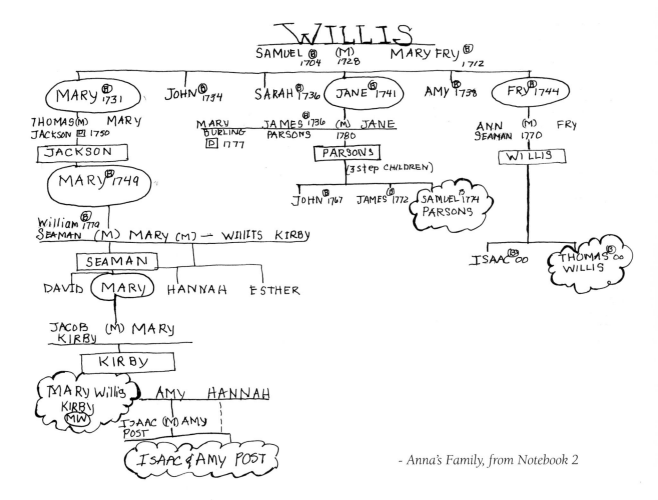

- Anna's Family, from Notebook 2

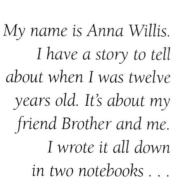

My name is Anna Willis.
I have a story to tell
about when I was twelve
years old. It's about my
friend Brother and me.
I wrote it all down
in two notebooks . . .

Introduction –
My Name Is Anna Willis

My name is Anna Willis. I have a story to tell about when I was twelve years old. It's about my friend Brother and me. I wrote it all down in two notebooks, so I wouldn't forget anything Brother told me. It was like a mystery story, revealed little by little on our weekly visits. Ever since childhood, I've usually been the first to rise in the morning. I would tiptoe down the stairs so that no one would hear me. As I sneaked into the kitchen and turned on the light I was always greeted by this mysterious verse that a relative had long ago carefully cross-stitched on white linen, and that's now mounted above the kitchen table. I did not realize then that each day, those words helped set a course for my young life to pursue—starting with my friendship with Brother. Here is the verse. . . .

The runaway
slave came to my
place he stopt
outside.
He stayed with
me a week before
He recuperated
and pass'd north
M.W., 1850

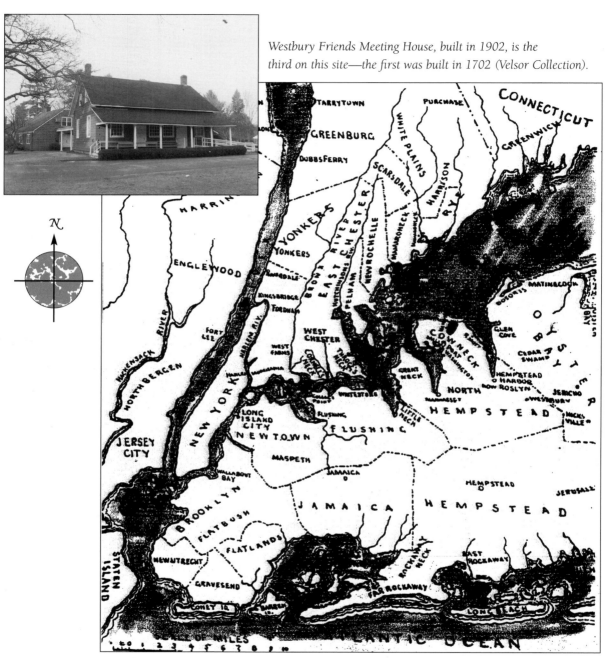

Westbury Friends Meeting House, built in 1902, is the third on this site—the first was built in 1702 (Velsor Collection).

Map of western Long Island showing Westbury, Jericho, and nearby Roslyn Harbor—said to be an 1830-50 Underground Railroad departure point for New York and Connecticut and other points north, as well as for eastern Long Island (1890 Map of Western Long Island, New York and Part of Westchester County, Thomas C. Cornell).

Nameplate for The New-York Gazette and the Weekly Mercury, in which the account of Thomas Jackson's escape was published c 1763. This reprint was compiled by the Queens Historical Society with advertisements from 1760-1763 (Queens Historical Society Collection).

children, my wife and I, and she's passed on, so maybe sometime you could help me write about these stories. Anyway, my grandfather found this clipping in some papers saved by his family, and he thinks it is the story of my father's great-great-grandfather." Brother adjusted his wire-rimmed glasses just a little before he read from the passage.

The notes are about this announcement in the *New-York Gazette*, dated July 18, 1763," Brother began. "Now New York, for more than a hundred years, Anna, had slaves just like the rest of the colonies. And historians know that some of these slaves were bought and sold right down on what today is called Wall Street—among the first 'commodities' to be sold there. Everything looked a little different then, of course. Wall Street ran inland from the waterfront, where ships came and went bringing supplies from Europe and the West Indies to New York and the other colonies.

To Be Sold

A NEGRO MAN, **29 years of age** precisely, who has been born in this country in a sober and regular family, and has never been in one of a different character. He has been accustomed to all sorts of work, but in his last service has been chiefly employed in the kitchen garden, as well as in family and table attendance. He can be fully recommended for honesty and sobriety.

THE PURCHASER MUST BE OF KNOWN SOBRIETY AND GOOD CHARACTER, WHO LIVES NOT ABOVE TEN MILES FROM STATEN-ISLAND. The reason of this limitation is that the wife of the Negro Man For Sale now lives there, and after many attempts, he has failed in getting her brought nearer to his present residence. His being offered to sale is an act of humanity in this matter.

For further particulars, apply to JOHN BROOME, Merchant in New-York.

Richard Wright's Gazette advertisement.

"Anyway, back to the story. Slaves were considered the property of their owners. Just as Fox belongs to you and the black lamb belongs to Mr. Spry. Sometimes slaves were set free by their masters. This was called manumission. That simply means 'to be set free.' And that was not usually the case. But if they *were* set free, they were given a paper that confirmed their freedom. Former slaves were to carry the paper wherever they went. Sometimes the Dutch slave masters would give a slave a pass so that he could travel around—it's too complicated to explain now. But that was all before the English arrived in New York in 1664. You remember your history, don't you?"

"Sure," I said. "What do you want to know? That date of the *Gazette* article—1763—is still way before the Revolutionary War. Is that what you mean?"

"Yes, that's what I was getting at," Brother replied. "Now as we said, slavery had been around for over a hundred years. But when a slaveholder could no longer take care of a slave—he just didn't have the money for food and clothing—he oftentimes would ask the slave to go find another master. Sometimes slaves would just run away instead. And I guess that's what happened to my father's great-great-grandfather, Thomas. When he was freed, he took his master's name as his own last name. The story seems to be that his master Isaac Jackson, who was a shopkeeper in New York City, died of natural causes in 1763—the year of the *Gazette* article. He being a man of means, he had a will. In his will he stated . . . here it is," he said, reading from the old newspaper account:

RUNAWAY

On the 30th of January 1778, a negro boy named Alick, about fifteen years of age. Had on when he went away: a check shirt, reddish coloured jacket, breeches, stockings and hat. He is branded on the breast with the letters **R.W.**

Whoever will secure said boy, or give information of any person or persons harbouring him, shall receive Four Dollars reward from **Richard Wright** in George Street, No. 22.

All Masters of Vessels are forbid harbouring, or carrying off the said boy on their peril.

Richard Wright's Gazette advertisement.

> Set at Liberty a Mullatto slave called Thomas Jackson, and provided Security to render his Manumission effectual.

I was amazed. Here was a newspaper story almost two hundred years old, and it was about Brother's family. I waited for him to say more.

"Oh, I forgot to mention," Brother continued. "After the slave revolt of 1712—and that's a whole other story I can tell you when you're older—people were afraid former slaves would cause problems for white slave owners. So the powers that be—the New York Colonial Assembly, they were called—passed rules to be sure the revolt couldn't happen again. The rule stated that in order to manumit a slave the master would have to post two bonds worth two hundred pounds each—to cover expenses the former slave might have in his lifetime. Newly freed slaves of course had no assets, so without the bonds, if they incurred a debt they could be sold to pay off the debt—a real or made-up one. The bond was kept by a third party just in case the slave should have trouble in the future.

"Well, evidently, no one could seem to find the bonds for Thomas Jackson even though he hadn't ever been in trouble. It was just the memory of the slave revolt and everyone was fearful. And there's more, Anna.

"Here it is," Brother continued.

> *But the Bond for that purpose hath been destroyed, and an unjust Attempt lately made to sell him at Vendue . . .*

"That's just a fancy word for auction," Brother said.

> *. . . which induced certain Persons, from Motives of Humanity, to indemnify the city of place in which he may reside . . .*

"Here they're just explaining what the bond was for," Brother explained.

> *. . . whereby his Freedom is protected.*

"Oh! So he was set free?" I asked.

"Well actually, no, the writer of the announcement is saying . . . you want me to read it again?"

"No, go on. I believe you."

"Let's see—"

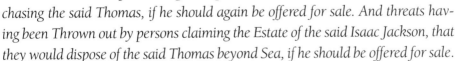

I was amazed. Here was a newspaper story almost two hundred years old, and it was about Brother's family.

> *T*hese [announcements] are therefore to caution all persons against purchasing the said Thomas, if he should again be offered for sale. And threats having been Thrown out by persons claiming the Estate of the said Isaac Jackson, that they would dispose of the said Thomas beyond Sea, if he should be offered for sale.

"Sounds as though the family was trying to keep Thomas from being sold back into slavery, doesn't it?—so they could keep him as their own 'property.' Kind of like fighting over the will just the way folks do today."

"Yes, it sure does sound like that," I said.

" 'That they would dispose of the said Thomas beyond Sea'," Brother read again. "In other words, Thomas wouldn't be considered free wherever he went—even beyond the sea. My ancestor. I am sad for him.

"And here it is, the final note:"

Masters of Vessels are prohibited from carrying him off as they will answer it at their peril, the Persons who have taken him into their Protection being Resolved to procure him justice. He is about 10–14 Years of age, five feet high, a slender Male, born in this country, and can read and write.

"So what happened to him, Brother?" I blurted out. "He was alone in a city run by white men. Where could he hide? He was young. I mean, my own brother can't do *anything* for himself, let alone work! Did Thomas go back to his family's house?"

We really don't know for sure," Brother said. "There's one thing I forgot to mention, Anna. Thomas probably had no idea who his parents were. Children were sold as slaves at an early age. Thomas could have been Isaac's slave for his whole life and never have known any member of his natural family. Kind of like your lamb. Taken and raised by another family. So when Thomas was age ten he knew no one except Isaac's friends and business partners. So I guess that's why my father had this notion that Isaac Jackson must have been a Quaker. You know about the Quakers, don't you?"

"Not much, really." I answered. "I do know that Father said his family members were originally Quakers, and that's why they settled on Long Island. But now we're all Methodist. So I guess you could say I don't know too much about that subject. What difference would it make to be a Quaker?"

"Early on in our history, the Quakers came to Long Island to escape religious persecution," Brother quietly explained. "They came in the mid-1600s and settled in Westbury, Oyster Bay, Jericho, and Flushing. They believed that a person did not need a minister to understand the teachings of the Bible. They would read the Bible and gather together—in each other's homes at first, then in simple meeting houses. The Meeting members were part of 'The Society of Friends,' and called 'Quakers,' or just 'Friends.' Some Friends such as John Woolman and Elias Hicks spoke about how all men are equal in the sight of God."

"Brother, isn't that what the Declaration of Independence is all about? That everyone is created equal?"

"Yes, in fact there were Quakers who helped to write that document. But unfortunately, it took around eighty-five years for people to understand that those words meant that slaves and former slaves were equal too. But there's something else in the suitcase, Anna. A copy of a speech I heard years ago made by Henry Hicks about the early history of the Quakers and Elias Hicks. The speech has a long name—it's called 'Freeing Slaves on Long Island by Members of the Society of Friends and Quakers and Self-Help Organizations Among Colored People,' and it is dated January 9, 1941. Henry Hicks mentions that the Quakers were the first group to speak up about the inequality of slavery on Long Island. In 1775, Elias Hicks met with members of the Westbury Friends who owned slaves, and convinced them to manumit their slaves. Fifty-four slaves were set free right here by 1776." Pretty complicated, all this . . .

"But remember," Brother went on. "My father's great-great-grandfather Thomas was supposed to be freed in 1763. That would have been twelve years *before* Elias Hicks spoke out against slavery. But John Woolman had come through Long Island earlier and spoken against slavery too. So maybe that's one reason why Isaac decided to free Thomas. And if Isaac was a Quaker, then he would have done business with other Quakers. Maybe they helped Thomas find a place to work and live."

"Where do you think he went?" I asked.

"This is where the story seems to get a lit-tle sketchy," Brother answered. "I have a mem-oir that Thomas sort of put together when he was around ninety years old. I guess he had some time at that age to write down some

Thomas could have been Isaac's slave for his whole life and never have known any member of his natural family.

memories of his life. You know, older people sometimes do that. It usually takes some questioning grandchildren to motivate people to write things down. But by this time it was 1844, and many changes had taken place on Long Island—espe-cially in Westbury. So I guess Thomas decided to make some notes."

Brother paused and gave me a smile. "It must be time for you to go on home for lunch," he said. "Why don't we continue the story next week, Wednesday afternoon?" He placed the old newspaper article carefully back in the suitcase.

"You mean I have to wait a whole week till Wednesday to hear what hap-pened to Thomas?" I protested. "This is like watching TV. You just get into a story and it's continued later. Well, okay, Brother, it's a date. You own the Sweet Shop and have work to do and I have lots of summer chores. Next Wednesday it is."

As Fox and I walked back home, I realized for the first time how Brother's fam-ily history was different from mine. Father knew exactly who his relatives were and where they had come from long ago. We had an old family Bible that lists

everyone in the family starting from Westbury, England. I felt sad for Brother and for his ancestor Thomas Jackson. Maybe I shouldn't have said anything about the lamb. But if I hadn't, then Fox and I would never have heard about Thomas. Where would I go if I were ten and had no family? I stopped a moment at that thought, and rested on an old carriage stone on the edge of our property. I sat down quietly with my thoughts. Fox found a seat next to me. We thought together for a while.

"What do you think, Fox? Where would you go?" Fox's ears perked up. Wait a minute! That's easy, I said to myself. Fox always makes his way through people's back yards. He has shown me shortcuts. He has taken me places. Especially when I was coming home from school. Fox had a special talent for finding families that liked him. That's what I would do. I would go to someone I could trust, to a friend's house. But who would have been Thomas's friend? I guess it would have been just as Brother said—someone who did business with his master Isaac Jackson. I wonder. Would I go to Mr. Spry's house? How would I get there? There certainly weren't any cars way back in the 1760s. There were no trains. I guess people traveled by horse and buggy. In fact, that's what I'm sitting on. The step that people used ages ago to get into a carriage.

What kind of carriage could Thomas use? I know! Boy, now I'm thinking. I got it! A wagon. People would have brought their farm goods to the market by wagon. Maybe that's how Thomas knew someone like himself, a friend to help him. I wonder if slaves in 1763 were allowed to go to the market with the farm goods.

"I bet that's it, Fox." I said out loud. "Thomas knew other slaves and Quakers from working in the store with Mr. Isaac Jackson and somehow he found a way to live with another Quaker family. What do you think? Good idea? Fox! Fox, where are you? Just when the story was getting good."

Fox was nowhere to be found. As I broke my concentration I could smell what had attracted my friend. Lunchtime. I love the smell of bacon cooking . . . must be BLTs for our family's lunch.

July 20, 1955 –
Thomas's Escape
Two Hundred Years Ago

think mother was a bit surprised the following week when I turned down her offer of new shoes. It was Wednesday afternoon, time to visit Brother, and shoes could easily wait. I remember the last pair of shoes we bought—my red sneakers getting ready for summer. I loved them so much that when it came time to go to bed, I actually wore them to sleep in. The only problem was that the rubber soles tore the sheets. I woke up in a mess of white rags. But this time, shoes were less important than meeting Brother. I wanted to hear the rest of the story!

By the time Fox and I made our way up Clay Street, Brother was already sitting on the porch waiting with the old brown suitcase by his side. "Hi, Brother," I greeted him. "I've had a great deal of time to think about Thomas and I think he probably would have gone to a friend's house for safety, when they were trying to capture him."

"Easy, girl," said Brother. "How is an escaping slave—even a newly freed one—going to find a friend?

"Easy, girl," said Brother. "How is an escaping slave—even a newly freed one—going to find a friend? Remember, Thomas didn't have either the bonds or his manumission papers—both had been lost. Even more, how would ten-year-old Thomas have a friend in the first place?"

I told him my theory, explaining how Fox always navigated to people who fed him and talked to him and he managed to have friends all over town. Then I explained my theory about going to the market.

"Brother," I said. "Do you think slaves would have been allowed to go to the market with their owner? Or perhaps even just on their own? And just maybe, if Thomas had been working at Isaac Jackson's store his whole life, he could have made friends with one of the regular customers, couldn't he?"

"Sure," said Brother, "I have a lot of regular customers in my Sweet Shop. Some of them I talk to. Some folks I just say 'Nice day.' 'How is everything?' 'What do you think about the weather?', and so on. But, there are other folks I've known since I was a boy. We played on the same baseball teams in school. We go to church together. We talk about other things. Things we think are important."

We sat quietly for a moment, Brother and I. I didn't know what to say. Maybe I was rushing him to talk. So I sat and waited.

"You know, Anna," Brother finally said, clearing his throat, "I just hadn't given it much thought but you're probably right. Thomas lived above Isaac Jackson's store and surely knew all the customers. But who would have talked to him about things like this? About freedom? That's the part I have trouble putting together. Certainly another former slave would have talked to him. And maybe that's the connection. Here, let me read to you what Thomas wrote in his memoir and maybe we can put the pieces together."

Brother bent over in his chair and placed the brown suitcase on his lap. He clicked open the latches . . .

Brother bent over in his chair and placed the brown suitcase on his lap. He clicked open the latches and pulled out several other old pieces of paper with brown writing all over them. I couldn't see the print. I could see that the writing was very small, and the notes seemed to have been made at different times. Some of the ink was darker than in other places and some of the writing ran up the side of the papers and all around the edges. It looked like the way friends write in each others' autograph books today. You start thinking you have lots of room on the page and then you run out of space and you have no choice but to write up the side or even upside down and in the in-between spaces. Brother took a little time as he read to himself, and then he spoke.

"You know paper was really hard to come by in those days, Anna, so folks tended to write on every available inch. Sometimes that makes it hard to read today—old paper, ink faded in places, different handwriting from different times. Here it is. Forgive me for being so slow. Look here. Actually, I see that Thomas is a little vague about his means of escape after Isaac Jackson's death. I think he was vague for a number of reasons. One critical reason was that it was still only 1844 when he finally wrote this memoir—and maybe people were still afraid someone would find out their parents had assisted a fugitive slave and they could lose their property and be put in jail."

"But, Brother, eighty years after the fact?" I asked.

"Well, I don't know for sure about that. But you see . . . the families that helped slaves to escape actually helped for generations, until Lincoln's Emancipation Proclamation in 1863 and the end of the Civil War—and then finally ratification of the Thirteenth Amendment in 1865. So it just might have been that Thomas didn't want anyone to know the particulars of the route. It may have been the same in the 1840s as it was when he used it long ago. That's all I can figure. I mean, why go to the trouble to tell your story and then leave out the important parts? I think he probably felt he owed it to the families who helped him, not to be specific. Here, this is what he wrote about the days right after Isaac Jackson's death."

> *B*eing a small boy [in 1763] I was afraid of being taken by a mean master. So I went back to the street where Mr. Jackson had his store. I thought that if I was lucky I would find someone who would let me work for him. I hid in the back of Mr. M____'s store, behind some stacks of wood. I knew he was like Mr. Jackson, a kindly man. I hoped he would be kind to me. When Mr. M____ found me he told me I could not stay. It wasn't safe—there was notice of a reward for my capture. He was very generous. He fed me and gave me a pair of shoes to wear, and a coat. When a load of lumber came into the city from Long Island he told me to hide in the wagon on its return trip. I hid under a pile of supplies being loaded in the wagon for the trip home. The owner did not know I was there. A young slave boy hid me while he piled supplies all around me—cloth, clocks, boxes of goods—I was glad for the soft things. He took me east of the city all the way to Long Island and directed me to The Brush. I lived in The Brush at first and I worked nearby at the Jackson Mill. It turns out that the mill owner was a cousin of Isaac Jackson. There were many slaves there, some escaped former slaves like me. We stayed because there was work for us and Mr. Jackson was very generous and kind.

"Oh, what a wonderful story!, Brother. But I'm confused. Didn't Thomas already have a pair of shoes? Or a coat?" I also wondered what "The Brush" was, but decided to ask about that later.

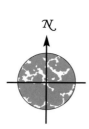

"The Brush," along the South Shore Jerusalem River near today's Bellmore Creek, safe haven for Thomas Jackson (Velsor Collection). . . .
The Jackson home in today's Wantagh, built in 1655, where Thomas lived while working in Mr. Jackson's mill (Velsor Collection).

"Child, things were different back then. Many slaves were not well clothed. Of course it would depend upon the family they lived with, and the economic conditions, and the work that the slaves were doing. But the truth is that a slave can't run far without shoes. I guess there really wasn't much guarantee of anything for slaves. No family, just their master."

"Brother, tell me about Mr. M___. Was that his name? Why did he give Thomas shoes? Why do you think he was more generous than Isaac Jackson?"

"Well, Anna, Mr. M___ probably knew Thomas could not safely stay with him, but that he could at least help him with his journey. To give him clothing was really a great act of kindness, don't you think?"

I thought a minute, remembering my conversation that morning with Mother. "Yes, it certainly is. I guess I sometimes forget. I mean, I just think that everyone is like me and has stuff. Brother, who was this Mr. M___? Do you know anything about him?"

Brother smiled and tamped down his pipe, puffed a little, and looked away into the distance as he seemed to gather his thoughts. "Mr. M___ wasn't his real name, I don't believe. When you're a little older maybe you'll want to read some of the well-known slave stories. These stories are called 'narratives.' Which means simply that some educated people wrote down the stories of certain slaves who escaped. The first stories were published and used to help young black children to understand their past. A Quaker woman named Abigail Mott lived in New York and wrote down some of these stories as early as the 1830s, and they were used for students in the African Free Schools in New York City. The point of all this is simply to say, that when you read the stories, the storytellers leave out the names of the actual slave owners as well as the people who helped them along the way. The names are simply referred to with an initial—generally a made-up one. That way a slave catcher couldn't find the name of the escaping slave, and of course no legal agency could ever trace the story to find the actual persons who might have helped the slave escape in the first place."

"Well, I guess things were pretty compli-cated," I said. "I mean, here you have some people helping slaves escape and other people wanting them back. There's a lot of mystery behind these stories. Why would one man see Thomas as a boy who needed a safe place to live, and another only want him for the work he could do?"

"It takes a special kind of person to have the courage to escape with no idea where he was going, don't you think, Anna? . . . I try to see events as people saw them long ago. History's more real to me this way."

Brother smiled over at me. I wondered, was it okay to ask him all these things?

"Well, that's the fun of reading history, Anna," he continued. "You and I can look at this event and see that poor Thomas was in trouble. But remember, it's 1955 now—almost two hundred years later. And we have the advantage of knowing that slavery was a terrible event in our nation's history, and that it ended officially just after the Civil War—even though strong feelings about that still continue to this day. But when Thomas was escaping he had no idea what events were in front of him or where he was going, or who his family would be. He had to rely solely on the judgment of Mr. M____. It takes a special kind of person to have the courage to escape with no idea where he was going, don't you think, Anna? I'm old now, and I've learned that it's important to try to see the whole picture of the times. To try to see events as people saw them long ago. History's more real to me this way."

We sat there a while. I didn't understand where Brother was going with his comments, yet I knew he needed to say what he did. I was dying to hear more. I waited for his thoughts to return before I asked my next question.

Brother, Thomas writes about The Brush. Where is it? I've never heard of a town with that name. Was it close to here in Westbury? Do you know anything about it?"

"Yes and no," Brother said, again with a smile. I was realizing that our friendship, Brother's and mine, was a pleasing one for us both.

"A few years ago I asked myself that question, Anna, and tried to find out where this spot was. It was not an easy task. I didn't really know where to start. I first looked at some old maps of Long Island, but I couldn't find it. Then I decided to look for Mr. Jackson, the man who did shelter Thomas and other escaped and former slaves—and offer them work at Jackson Mill—and that was much easier. John Jackson, I discovered, first came to Long Island from New England in 1653. He became a Quaker after he arrived and settled in the town of Hempstead. He had a son named John who petitioned for a sawmill on the Jerusalem River in 1687. This mill and the property surrounding it covered just about two hundred acres. Well, I had never heard of the Jerusalem River but I looked on the map again and there it was, right between what today is called Wantagh and North Bellmore. Down near Long Island's South Shore. Do you know where that is?"

"Brother," I said. "I have no idea! Is it far from where we are right now?"

"Well, have you ever been to Jones Beach?" Brother asked.

"Yes, Father has taken us there on special family occasions. Why?"

"Well, the road to Jones Beach goes right down along the Jerusalem River. Today it's known as Bellmore Creek. In fact, where the river meets the saltwater inlet on the South Shore, that's right where the mill used to be. You just travel down the Jones Beach Causeway—oh, that's right. It's hard to keep up with the names—now it's called the Wantagh Parkway. You know, just south of Sunrise Highway. If you look west toward New York City you can actually see the waterway that led to the place once called The Brush. It seems that before the Revolutionary War, escaped slaves and later free blacks lived in this area because of the protection offered by lots of short trees and thick undergrowth. At least that's the story that has long been told about The Brush."

So, what did Thomas do?" I asked eagerly. "Did he sign himself up as a slave to Mr. Jackson? Or as a former slave? Did he have any chance for freedom?"

"Not at first. He worked for the Jacksons for a modest wage and lived with other escaped slaves in a small house near the mill. You see, the Jacksons, just like other Long Island landowners, owned slaves. Slaves were used to build much of Long Island. They were a valuable part of the economy—in fact, census records show there were probably about four thousand slaves on Long Island around that time. It wasn't until the decade before the Revolution that these Quaker settlers really questioned the morality of slavery."

"So, when did Thomas get his freedom?" I asked. "What did he do? If Mr. Jackson didn't own him, then he couldn't set him free, right?"

Brother laughed—a friend-to-friend sound. "You seem to understand the problem very well, Anna. But I'm not surprised. I'll let you ponder that question for a while and see what you come up with. It's getting late. How about next Wednesday?"

Slaves were used to build much of Long Island. They were a valuable part of the economy . . .

Well, I knew there was no hope of hearing the rest of the story that day. I could tell Brother had made up his mind to hold on to it till next time. I smiled right back and jumped out of my chair. Fox jumped up too, ready for the walk home, tail wagging as always when the next adventure begins.

"Thanks, Brother. This has been fun!" I said, giving him a big hug. "Sure I'll be back, and I think I'll start writing some things down so I don't forget all you've told me. See you Wednesday. Come on, Fox, let's see what's for supper tonight." And down the steps we went. What a day!

As I left, I looked back and saw that Brother had not moved. He was sitting in his green wicker rocking chair on the porch, reading his father's great-great-grandfather's memoir as if for the first time. He seemed older than I remembered. He was much taller than my father, but somehow now seemed shorter sitting alone with his thoughts. He didn't raise his head as Fox and I slipped behind the hedge and walked down the sidewalk toward home.

"Fox," I said. "What am I going to say to Mother about the shoes? I mean, here she is trying to be nice and I was not the least bit interested. I know, I'll just say that, and apologize. Maybe I'll even tell her about my amazing Wednesday afternoon visits with Brother."

As it happened I did tell her I was sorry about the shoes and she just smiled and tousled my hair. I told her about my visits with Brother too, but not the *reason* yet—I'll tell her when I know the whole story. . . .

"It takes a special kind of person to have the courage
to escape with no idea where he was going, don't you think, Anna?
I'm old now, and I've learned that it's important to try to
see the whole picture of the times. To try to see events as people
saw them long ago. History's more real to me this way."

July 27, 1955 – The Move From Mr. Jackson's Mill

ednesday again! Weekday mornings in the summer usually meant that there were lots of chores to be done by the three of us—tending the garden, cleaning up our rooms, helping our mother with special tasks. I'm always glad to do them, but today I decided to avoid other assignments and to retreat to my room and reorganize my stuff.

The morning kind of dragged on. It was very warm indoors—hot and humid. I suddenly thought of a small notebook I had saved for English class. It looked new. I had never used it. I labeled it "Brother and Me." I started to write down some of the things that Brother had told me about Thomas Jackson. It was so warm I guess I fell back to sleep. All I could think of was how Thomas was left to

I suddenly thought of a small notebook I had saved for English class. It looked new. . . . I labeled it "Brother and Me."

take care of himself and how he still was not free just because some papers had gotten lost. What would happen if someone found out about him? Would he be forced to leave the Jackson Mill? I dreamt about what the old mill looked like. It didn't look like much fun for a young boy. Life must have been rough.

When I finally woke up and got myself together again, I realized it was already lunchtime and that meant I could soon go see Brother again.

Fox was waiting patiently for me in the back yard under the maple tree. He had this funny habit of digging a hole in the shade of the tree, and sleeping as if he were in a nest. Father said he liked to cool off that way. All I knew was, I had to make sure Fox did a good job of shaking himself off before we went up the street to Brother's.

"Shake, shake, shake," I said "It's finally time to hear more of the story, Fox. Are you up for a walk?" Without hesitation Fox leapt out of his cooling spot, shook himself off just as I expected, and started walking straight across the lawn and down the sidewalk toward Brother's house. He knew exactly where we were going!

"I like your new blue sneakers," said Brother, as Fox and I approached his yard side by side.

"Thanks. Mother and I talked about the shoes and then we went shopping for some new clothes for camp too. Remember I went last summer? I had such a great time that I'm going for two weeks in August. I can't wait! Boy, it's really a hot day here, isn't it?"

"I think it's the hottest day we've had since last year," Brother said. "Come on up. I've made us some nice cold lemonade just for the occasion. I love lemonade with the fresh lemons on top. But I can still see some of the seeds, so watch out. Have a seat. And here's some water for our friend Fox."

Lemonade! Perfect right after lunch, perfect on this hottest day of days. I was sure grateful to Brother. So was Fox, whose tongue was lap-lap-lapping over his dish.

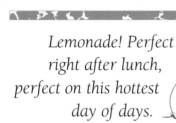

Lemonade! Perfect right after lunch, perfect on this hottest day of days.

"So, where are we going to find Thomas today?" I said. "I had this dream that he was working and something happened. That he couldn't stay at Mr. Jackson's Mill anymore. Is that what happened? Was he ever actually free?"

Brother looked pleased at my interest in the story. "Do you ever stop thinking about Thomas?" he asked, sipping on his lemonade. I could see he was eager to tell me more.

Not often," I replied. "I started to write down the story in an old notebook I had lying around my room. And as I was writing, I started to think about Thomas still not being free even though Isaac Jackson issued his manumission papers—and the bond and everything somehow got lost. So, if he wasn't free, was he at least safe?" Brother looked at me and started up the story again.

"Well I guess that's all a matter of opinion. I mean, Fox is safer living with you than he would be living alone in the woods, right?"

"Sure," I replied. "Living with us he has food and lots of love and a safe place to hide under the maple tree. But I know he'd certainly leave and find another home if he didn't like Clay Street anymore. That's actually how Fox came to us in the first place; he just appeared at the door one morning and stayed. Father put a few ads in the paper but no one seemed interested. So we called him Fox because he has a furry tail like a fox. He's been here ever since. He does have a mind of his own, and I hope he never leaves. I love him a whole lot. Right, Fox?"

Drawing of "The Old Mott House," built c 1715 in Cow Neck (today Port Washington), suggests the Long Island farmhouse landscape in pre-Revolutionary years (Queens Historical Society Collection).

Fox knew we were talking about him. His tail thump-thumped on the porch floor. During the discussion he had come up and managed to sit between Brother and me, as he eyed our pitcher of lemonade. I think he was waiting for his treat. Brother reached into the pocket of his blue seersucker pants and pulled out a special dog treat for Fox, who munched it right down.

"Well, in a way what Fox did with your family is what Thomas had to do," Brother said, just like that.

"You lost me." I said. "You mean, find a new home? Why?"

"Well, it seems there weren't that many Jacksons that weren't related. Here, let me find this memoir. I read on a little after you left last week. It seems that Isaac Jackson—Thomas's master in New York City who had died and freed him in his will—was actually a cousin of the Jacksons on Long Island. It wouldn't have made that much difference, because the mill was way out in Queens County, except that Mr. Jackson's cousin came out from New York to visit one hot Sunday afternoon. Thomas recognized him as someone he had known—a relative of his former master Isaac Jackson. And Thomas didn't know what the cousin knew about his escape."

Brother rested his lemonade glass on a little wicker table beside his chair and picked up the brown suitcase again. He slowly unlatched it and pulled out the same old brown sheets he had read from the week before.

"Here it is," Brother said, as he pointed to a line in one of the sheets.

Everything was going all right until one Sunday afternoon in the middle of summer, when a small group of visitors came out from the city. I was resting in the shade of a large tree when I saw the carriage coming down the road. I slipped behind the tree's wide trunk and peeked around to see who was coming, when I saw my old master's cousin and his family. At the time I wasn't sure if the new Mr. Jackson had told them that I was there. I decided to go hide in The Brush until I knew—it wasn't too far away. I walked casually in the other direction so no one would take notice of me. I stayed away for two days until it started to rain. I figured no one was looking for me. I would have been told or found. I returned to the cabin where we lived. That's when I heard that Mr. Jackson had come looking for me. I was very scared. I didn't know what to do.

"Safe is a personal term, Anna. I think he felt relieved. Just the sight of his former master's relative had set him on the run."

"Did he have to run away, Brother?" I said. "Just when things looked so good for him. Now he was alone again. Does this trouble ever end?"

"Well, I think he felt pretty helpless," Brother replied. "But he had to trust someone, so I guess he decided he didn't have much choice but to find out what Mr. Jackson knew."

I found Mr. Jackson up near the house later that afternoon and approached him with caution. He was happy to see me. He called me "son." It seems that his cousin was still looking for his "property" but he had no idea I was there.

Mr. Jackson had made arrangements for me to leave the mill. He said it was for my own safety. He didn't know whether his cousin would find out about me or not, but he knew he might come back. Mr. Jackson said that his wife came from the Seaman family of Jericho, and that they needed help and would be fair to me. I knew I had no choice. That was in the summer of 1770. Mr. Jackson and his wife took me in the wagon half a day's ride to Jericho, where I lived with Mr. Jonathan Seaman, who was a Quaker. He already owned two slaves.

"That's really exciting!" I exclaimed. "Is that the same town as the one next to ours? Or was it somewhere else?"

"Yes, it's the same town," Brother said. "Only it looked a lot different then. Thomas wrote a pretty interesting description of the town. Listen to this."

> *I was very surprised to see everyone plainly dressed. They did not look like the people in New York. They spoke to each other in a kind way. They always referred to each other as "thee" or "thou." The village had its own source of water and people grew their own vegetables. They had farm animals too. The farmers lived very well. I felt safe.*

"Brother, does that mean that Thomas finally *is* safe?" I asked.

Brother was silent a moment before answering me. "Safe is a personal term, Anna. I think he felt relieved. Just the sight of his former master's relative had set him on the run. Naturally, that left a lasting impression in his mind, and Thomas never forgot that moment. He never forgot the fear of being caught and the loneliness of running away. He never forgot the kindness that the Jackson family showed him, and later the Seaman family. I know this from reading these papers. Yes, he eventually felt safe. And he later helped others like himself."

"Brother, you're teasing me again!" I replied. "You have this amazing way of hinting about the next events. But you say he still isn't free. How does he ever *become* free?"

"Well, an interesting chain of events happened in Jericho in the 1770s," Brother explained. "And these events were the turning point in Thomas's life. Jericho was by then a prosperous village. It had a regular source of spring water that allowed for plentiful fresh water for everyone, as Thomas mentioned. The spring-fed pond sat right in the middle of the village. I remember it as a child—it was right in front of what's now the Milleridge Inn, before the road was widened.

"This pond was surrounded by a small picket fence to keep the farm animals from wandering in and out of it. The village houses were all gray shingled. None of them had paint—the cedar shingles were just allowed to weather to a mellow gray, so they seemed more a part of the landscape than houses do today. Next to the pond was what was called a "whitening yard" on the Willets' farm. My grandmother used to tell me that they bleached their linen out in the sunlight of the yard. Incidentally, Anna, linen is a very important commodity to the families who lived in Jericho. It's made from flax. Do you know what that is?"

"You've got me on that one, Brother," I said. "Sounds kind of like breakfast cereal!"

He laughed out loud at my silly remark, and pointed to a row of blue colored flowers blooming near his hedge. "There it is over there," he said. "Flax is a flowering plant that comes back every year. Villagers here and elsewhere relied on it—it is harvested, dried, and then separated into its natural fibers, and spun into cloth for dresses and shirts, and sheets and pillowcases for their beds. The seeds were used for oil."

"That's totally amazing!" I said. "How did the Quakers ever know that, Brother?"

"Just generations of farming tradition, I guess," he answered. "You know, mothers would teach their children and on it would go from one family to the next, along with their values and their Quaker traditions."

"So that's why they had to bleach the linen?" I said. "Because the dried fibers were kind of light brown?"

"Yes," replied Brother. "And they needed the water so they didn't make holes in the soft fabric as they completed the sunlight bleaching process. The linen would be made into bedsheets, clothing, and oftentimes samplers. Each of the sheets was then marked with an initial, dated in the finest cross-stitching—the mothers taught these special types of stitches to their daughters, generation to generation."

Brother sat back in his chair, and poked around in his pipe to get it started again. I thought some more about the smell of his tobacco. It always makes me feel he is content about something, whatever it is. He smiled again and puffed on his pipe.

"You know, the linen is a very important part of this story, Anna. I'd never really thought about it but these Quaker women made a great deal of linen and used it in all sorts of interesting ways. I'm sure the early female slaves helped in the process too. In fact I think that's where Thomas fell in love with my father's great-great-grandmother Sallie."

"What do you mean?" I said. "They worked together as slaves?"

"Well, yes and no," Brother replied. "I think I'm getting ahead of myself here."

"You mean you just like hiding the good parts?" I asked.

"Something like that," he said with a boyish grin on his weathered old face.

Brother paused and collected his thoughts. "I want to tell you this part first. You see, the Quakers didn't want to pay taxes because they didn't believe they should be held responsible for the salary of the local minister in the town; the minister wasn't Quaker and they didn't attend his church. Thomas wrote something about that—how the tax collectors would come around looking for payment, and instead they would take anything of value. Here it is." He paused, and followed the memoir by running his finger slowly along one line and then the next. "I told you that part. . . . Here's the part about the linen and hiding places."

I wanted to know everything, but I didn't want our visits to stop. Was Thomas free at last?

The Quaker women would hide their linen and other things of value from the collectors. Many of the houses and barns had secret cupboards or hidden rooms in their houses where they would put their valuables for safekeeping.

"These are pretty surprising pieces of history," I said. "Can you believe the tax collectors just took whatever they wanted?"

"Well, that's why I want you to write all this down, Anna. You see, now that I'm telling this story I'm seeing things just a little differently. So I'm glad you'll help by keeping a record. How far along are you?" he asked. "Keeping up?"

Actually, Brother, I did lots more this morning. I've written about everything you've told me so far about Thomas. Now I need to add today's part of the story. Is this almost the end?" I asked. I wanted to know everything, but I didn't want our visits to stop. Was Thomas free at last? Was the story complete?

"Heavens no, child! This is when the story really starts to get exciting. See you next Wednesday, but remember to add all this information to your notebook. I don't want to forget any of our discoveries."

"Where does the time go, Brother? We're going to be late for supper and I don't want Mother to wonder what's keeping me."

I jumped out of my seat and gave Brother a big kiss good-bye. I love the smell of the smoke from his pipe. It reminds me of my grandfather.

"Bye, Brother, please don't forget any part of the story—especially the part about your father's great-great-grandmother, Sallie." I said. "I want to know all about her!"

Fox had jumped to his feet, probably because he thought I was about to step on his tail and he wanted to avoid any conflict. We stepped off the porch and I waved good-bye. I saw Brother placing the old brown memoir sheets back in the suitcase, where they would stay for the next seven days waiting to be explored one more time. Fox did his own exploring on the way home—sniff here, investigate there, but always heading for home.

As Fox and I walked into the kitchen that night, I looked at the verse stitched in linen and hung on the wall so long ago. I just couldn't help but wonder if the message had been sewn in Jericho. On the top right-hand side it said "M.W., 1850." But "the runaway slave came to my house he stopt outside. . . ." it said. Was M.W. someone who helped escaping slaves like Thomas? Who exactly was M.W.? Was she someone from my own family? What a thought! I vowed to find out. . . .

August 3, 1955 –
Life in Old Jericho

hy do summer days seem so long? Maybe because there really isn't enough to do, so time just drags on. This week seemed longer than usual. I had hoped I could talk Father into a family trip to Jones Beach. He said he was too busy during the week, and that there were just too many people at the beach on the weekends. I wasn't really seeking a swimming outing as much as finding the place where Thomas had hidden so long ago before coming to the Seamans' house in Jericho. Did "The Brush" even still exist? I would have to work on this subject. Maybe something would turn up. You never know.

I started to think about the early Quakers, about the Seaman family. I wondered what they had looked like, . . . what their lives were like.

Fox and I were a little early on Wednesday. Brother wasn't there. No black Buick parked in the driveway. So Fox and I decided to wait on the porch. As we waited I started to think about the early Quakers, about the Seaman family. I wondered what they had looked like, how they dressed, what their lives were like. I must remember to ask Mother if I could go to the library and get a book on Quakers so I could have a better idea.

At that thought, Brother arrived. With a sharp bump off the curb and a quiet purr of the engine he drove his car up the drive all the way into the garage. He opened the door and emerged carrying a pile of library books and the old brown suitcase. I laughed. We were even beginning to think alike!

"Anna," he said, "I'm sorry I'm late. Glad you two waited. You see, I thought it might be important to our story if you could see some pictures of old Jericho, Westbury, and Oyster Bay. I also thought you might like to see a picture of the Quakers that Thomas talks about in his memoir."

"Oh, thanks, Brother!" I said, as he handed me an assortment of old books from the Westbury Library. I felt pretty excited at the thought of learning what my own town was like so long ago. We sat down together on the porch.

"While I was in the library I found this book that mentions Elias Hicks," Brother said. He picked up the book and turned the pages till he came to a picture of a small house with a front porch and small windows. Under the picture the caption read "The home of Elias Hicks, who came to Jericho in 1771 to live with Jonathan Seaman after marrying his daughter Jemima. He was a Quaker preacher and lived in Jericho for fifty years."

"Wait a minute, Brother," I said. "Is this the same Seaman family that Thomas Jackson came to work for?"

"Yes, it is," Brother said. "Thomas writes about it—and that's exactly why I went to the library this morning!"

"You mean Elias Hicks actually owned slaves?" I said. I could hardly believe it.

> *"The first year or so was quiet. I worked at the Seaman house with two slaves, _____ . . ."*

"Not actually, no," said Brother, "because the slaves belonged to his father-in-law. Remember, Thomas said he was going to work for Jonathan Seaman and that was 1770. Well, according to Thomas, Mr. and Mrs. Seaman didn't live very long after Elias arrived. Maybe that's why Jemima and Elias came to live in Jericho after they were married—to take care of her parents. I can't tell from these papers. But soon after Elias came, Jemima's parents died and gave all their 'property' to their daughter and son-in-law Elias Hicks. Thomas talks about this. Here, let me see if I can find where he mentions them. Brother picked up his brown suitcase, clicked open the latches, and carefully pulled out the memoir papers. He pointed to a faded line and began to read. . . ."

The first year or so was quiet. I worked at the Seaman house with two slaves, _____ . One of my tasks was to smoke the meat in the smokehouse to keep it for the winter months. I worked hard, but I was never lonely. The family took good care of me. The three of us lived in a room off the kitchen of their house.

In 1771 or thereabouts, Jemima, their daughter, married a man named

Elias Hicks and not long after that everything changed. Mr. and Mrs. Seaman died two years later, and Mr. Seaman's will stated that his slaves should be given to his daughter Jemima and his son-in-law Elias Hicks, along with his other possessions and his home, and that is what happened.

Well, that was the same year, 1773, when the Quakers at the Yearly Friends Meeting in Flushing directed that any Friends holding slaves would be disowned if they "continued to buy or sell Negroes." The Friends also said that slaves should be set free according to certain rules. If a slave was a woman she could be free at eighteen and a man at twenty-one.

It seems Elias didn't much care about my age; nobody knew I was only nineteen at the time and you had to be twenty-one to be free. But there were still Quakers in Jericho who kept their slaves even though they weren't supposed to. So Elias Hicks in 1775 was appointed by the Yearly Meeting to visit families who still had slaves, and convince them to manumit their slaves.

Elias worked really hard. He traveled to people's homes and by the end of that year he was responsible for fifty-four slaves being freed. By 1791 he was given credit for one hundred fifty-four manumissions. . . .

"Thomas is finally free!, right?" I said.

"I believe so, Anna—at last!" said Brother. "But Thomas never said he was set free, and it must be that he *was* freed again through the kind acts of Elias Hicks. Thomas just never comes out and states it in his memoir. I don't know why. But take these books home and read about the Quakers if you want to. I know they're all adult books, but the pictures are good. See this one here? This is a picture of Elias Hicks himself. He wasn't always this old! There are only two known pictures of him, and this is the most famous one. He looks really serious, doesn't he?"

"Scary, Brother!" I said. "Now let me get this story straight. He was the one responsible for persuading the local Quakers to free their slaves?"

Portrait of Elias Hicks (1748-1830; Richard Gachot Collection).

realized. The hedge in front of the Ellis house was thick but I could certainly hear the two German shepherds as they raced around the side of the house, barking at Fox—who just ignored them as he always does. Thomas had turned out to be lucky after all, I realized, as I brought my thoughts back to my assignment. I wonder what he did next? Where he lived? And if he really was finally free?

★ ★ ★

Well, that was the same year, 1773, when the Quakers at the Yearly Friends Meeting in Flushing directed that any Friends holding slaves would be disowned if they "continued to buy or sell Negroes." The Friends also said that slaves should be set free according to certain rules. If a slave was a woman she could be free at eighteen and a man at twenty-one. . . . But there were still Quakers in Jericho who kept their slaves even though they weren't supposed to. So Elias Hicks in 1775 was appointed by the Yearly Meeting to visit families who still had slaves, and convince them to manumit their slaves. Elias worked really hard. He traveled to people's homes and by the end of that year he was responsible for fifty-four slaves being freed. By 1791 he was given credit for one hundred fifty-four manumissions. . . .

★ ★ ★

August 10, 1955 –
Lunch With Brother

uesday it rained all day. That was okay, because I needed to finish the books Brother had given me, and I also needed to write down the rest of our conversation from last week. My brother and sister were off visiting friends so I had no come-play-with-us distractions.

As I opened the picture book I couldn't believe the drawings of early Long Island. There was a map dated 1859, showing a few roads and names of people's houses. I looked for Elias Hicks's house. There wasn't any Hicks family in Jericho named Elias—there was only a Valentine Hicks house. That's funny, I thought. Didn't Brother mention Valentine Hicks and his fields? Was that the Valentine Hicks who married Elias's daughter? I'll have to remember to ask Brother about this Valentine person.

Then I found a picture of the Maine Maid Inn!

Next I found a house labeled "Jackson farm," a little south of Jericho. Was that where Thomas Jackson finally lived? Then I found a picture of the Maine Maid Inn!

It looked like a fairly new photograph—at least far newer than the others. It had two wings that could have been added on to the original house. This was a different picture from the one Brother had shown me before. Was it because of the parking lot that now surrounded the house? I really need to straighten all this out with Brother.

That's when the telephone rang. I could hear Mother's voice from downstairs.

"It's fine with me," she said. "Just a minute, Brother. I'll ask Anna to come to the telephone."

I jumped off my bed and went to pick up the phone out in the hall. I paused a moment, hoping he wasn't canceling our meeting for Wednesday. "Hi, Brother. This is Anna. Everything okay?"

"Oh, yes!" said Brother. I could hear the background noise of the people in his shop. A lady was asking about sour drops from England. "Anna, I just had a nice conversation with your mother. She gave me permission to ask you to lunch tomorrow. Can you come?"

"Lunch?" I asked.

"Yes, I thought maybe you'd like to go with me to the Maine Maid Inn," he said.

I couldn't believe it—the Maine Maid Inn! "Sounds like a wonderful idea," I said. "I'd love that! I'll meet you at your house. What time?"

"How about our usual time, one o'clock?" Brother said.

"It's a date. I'll see you then. And thanks, Brother. This sounds like so much fun!"

I guess I'll have to dress up, I said to myself as I hung up the telephone. The Maine Maid Inn—somehow, part of the story! And I was about to find out why.

Here was the chance to wear my blue dress again—the one Mother had made for me for the spring concert at school. I loved the dress—it was blue and white checks with pink roses, and the front was hand-sewn smocking.

Visitors on the lawn of the Valentine Hicks House, built in 1789 and today the Maine Maid Inn (Jericho Public Library Historical Collection).

The next day I got all ready in plenty of time—blue dress, hair brushed and up in a ribbon. I had a little trouble finding my shoes. One was under my bed and the other was stuck behind my old sneakers in the back of the closet I shared with my sister. But find them I did, and off we went, Fox and I.

As I walked up the street with the library books under my arm, I smiled at what a great summer I had found in my talks with Brother. He was right there at home waiting for us.

Hi! You're looking very stylish today, Anna. And so are you, old friend," he said as he patted Fox on the head. They shook hands as usual.

"I'll bet you're wondering why I asked you to come to lunch with me," Brother remarked.

"Actually I was wondering why you spoke to Mother about it first," I said. "How come?"

"I didn't want your parents to be upset with me," Brother said. "You see, it's just that some people think folks like me should not be seen with folks like you. We're different in color, and I just didn't want your mother and father to be upset. I mean, even though it's 1955 there are still some folks that turn their heads at such things. Your father is important in town and I just didn't want anything to come of it. I made sure the Maine Maid Inn would welcome us, too."

I sure didn't know what to say to this new thought. Mother and Father had certainly never mentioned anything about it. "Brother, you mean like our black lamb?" I said. "That's pretty silly! I thought things were different now."

He smiled at me and I smiled back. We walked to the car without saying a word.

"You know, Brother, I've learned that when someone invites you out it's usually because they want to have a happy time. I know you've been talking about this restaurant, and now you've made me curious. I think there's something more to it than just lunch. Am I right?"

"You'll see," Brother said as he opened the passenger's side door and let Fox jump in the back seat while I got to sit in the front. There was some mystery happening here. I noticed the brown suitcase neatly tucked behind the driver's seat.

Jericho is only a few minutes' ride from Westbury, so we were there before I knew it. Brother parked in the shade of an old locust tree. He took the brown suitcase from the car. We left the windows open a little for Fox and climbed out of the car, but we didn't go into the restaurant at first. Brother led the way around to one side of the restaurant and pointed to the house across the street.

"See that house, Anna?" he said. "That's Elias Hicks's house. I don't know why it's painted a mustard yellow color, because back then it would have been just plain gray shingle. But this is his house, and on the left side, which looks a little older than the rest, is where the kitchen was. That was where Thomas stayed when he worked for the Seaman family. That's where my own father's

Home of Elias Hicks, Jericho, built in 1695, with adjacent barn. The house still stands on Old Jericho Turnpike near the Maine Maid Inn (John Butler).

great-great-grandfather used to live."

I just stood there, amazed by this connection to long ago—right before my eyes!

"Oh, Brother, this is so wonderful! It looks really old, but it doesn't look so different from the other houses around here. I mean, it looks old and run-down. But why isn't there a special sign or something? How are people supposed to know?"

Well, I don't think most people on Long Island even know who Elias Hicks was, Anna." Brother said, winking at me. "That may be left up to you— to tell the story." What a thought! *Me* telling people the story of Elias Hicks and how he changed people's lives in Westbury ages ago. I'd need to think about that—pretty important responsibility.

"Can we walk around and look at the house?" I asked.

"I don't think there'll be any problem," Brother said.

"How about the barn—was that here when Elias Hicks lived in the house?"

"I believe it's the same one," he said. "It's hard to tell. Next door on the south side is the original tavern and stagecoach stop for people traveling on Jericho Turnpike. The story goes that Elias used to let people stay at his house and sleep in the living room. He never asked anyone for money, but some people left money. He used all of it to help build the Jericho Friends Meeting House that's just east of where we're standing— it's been there since about 1787. Maybe you can see from over here," he said, as we walked back toward the restaurant. "Yes," he said. "It's right there. See it?"

I could see two old buildings just down the road. One was a little beige two-story house, and the other was smaller, with a little

The Jericho Friends Meeting House on today's Old Jericho Turnpike, built c 1787 (John Butler).

porch running all along one side. "Is it the little house or the bigger one?" I asked.

"It's the larger building that's further back on the property," he said, as he pointed to the beige shingled building that was nicely sheltered by a huge old oak tree.

"I remember that building!" I said. "I saw a picture of it in the book you let me borrow. There were people standing on the porch. They had on long dresses, and high-collared shirts and jackets. Was that some kind of Quaker Meeting? The kind you told me about?"

"Yes, Anna. That was a Sunday morning Meeting for Jericho Friends—a very important time in the week for the Quakers. They gather and sit mostly in silence, standing to speak if they wish to, thinking about things alone yet together. It's a beautiful Quaker custom that continues to this day," Brother said.

I thought about that. Sitting in silence, together. Kind of like what Brother and I do, sitting on the porch but not talking. It's kind of peaceful. A good time to just think about things.

"Which reminds me, Brother. I found a map in the book dated 1859, and I looked for Elias's house and he wasn't listed. Valentine Hicks had his house here. Who was that, his son?"

"No, Anna. It's a sad story. Elias and his wife Jemima had eleven children and unfortunately their four sons all died in their teens. No one knows why they died—perhaps some kind of illness. But they did have three daughters who lived. One of them, Abigail, married Valentine Hicks in 1804—that's the farmhouse with the bleaching yard I told you about. I have the family tree in the suitcase and we can figure out that story a little bit later."

"Wait a minute, Brother! Elias Hicks's daughter married a relative?" I said.

"Well, no," said Brother. "They had the same last name but they actually came from completely different families in England so it was acceptable. Valentine was related to Henry Hicks—the same Hicks family that owns the nursery in Westbury today. And Valentine Hicks is the one that Hicksville is named after—he was president of the Long Island Rail Road in the 1830s. It's all pretty complicated."

"How do you know all this, Brother?" I asked.

"Well, I've been reading too and it's related to our story," he replied. "It seems that Valentine Hicks had worked in the city for a while as a shipper with his brother Isaac—we talked about him. Isaac built a home on Wheatley Road in about 1806. It's still there today—greatly changed but still right there all these generations later.

Isaac was older than Valentine. He started a small business in the city as a tailor. He kept reinvesting his money until he purchased lots of sailing ships he could use for trading out along Long Island Sound and back and forth from the city. Isaac employed his brother Valentine, and when they had made enough money they both left New York and came back out to Long Island. Valentine bought a farm here, and the Maine Maid Inn used to be his farmhouse. He employed men to help in the fields. Some of these men were former slaves, and some were said to be on the run."

"On the run," I asked. "What do you mean?"

"Thomas wrote a little story about Valentine Hicks and this house. I thought you might be interested in hearing about it. Come on, let's go inside and I'll tell you more," said Brother.

Brother opened the door to the restaurant and let me go inside first. The head waitress greeted us and asked us where we'd like to sit—upstairs or in the Hicks room. Brother asked for a seat in the upstairs room and off we went.

To get to our table we had to climb a long staircase that wrapped all around the front entrance hall. Up on the second floor we were seated at a small table near a window—with white tablecloth and sparkly silverware. There were a lot of people sitting and talking at different locations around the room. The waiter came over and welcomed us, and handed us each a menu. He asked Brother if everything was okay. Brother assured him that the seating was good.

"I always order the club sandwich," Brother said to me. "It comes with a nice heap of French fries!"

"Sounds good to me," I said. "And lemonade if they have any?"

"Same here," he said.

When the waiter returned Brother gave our order and returned the menus. Then Brother just started in talking as he always does.

"You see, Anna, according to Thomas, the story is that Valentine Hicks lived in this house and attended Jericho Meeting as a Quaker. He hired many people, as I said, to work on his farm. Thomas used to work for him during the harvest times. Most of the year I think he lived with the Seamans and worked on the dairy farm just south of here, but I can't really tell.

"Valentine Hicks . . . glanced out the window and saw one of his employees running across the field."

"On one particular morning—and this would probably have been during the harvest season when the farmers needed more help than usual—Valentine Hicks was sitting in his parlor working on his accounts, when he glanced out the window and saw one of his employees running across the field."

Brother reached down and put the little brown suitcase on an empty chair. He carefully unlatched it and pulled out Thomas's memoir. He read a bit, then turned the paper sideways, squinting his eyes. "It's funny how he seemed to have added this story to his writings a bit later," he said. "This particular one is written along the side of the page in very small print. He starts it right here, see?"

I leaned over the table and I could see where Thomas had carefully added this story along the border of one of his memoir pages.

"Why do you suppose he did that, Brother?" I asked. "Wrote it so small, and along the edge?"

"Two reasons I can think of. Either because paper was so hard to come by in those days, as you know, or he wanted to make the story a little less obvious just in case someone found the memoir. Remember, it was 1844 and Thomas feared that anyone found helping a slave could get into trouble. Here's the story.

V. H. made it a policy not to ask former slaves to identify whether they were legally free or not. Sometimes men would just come and ask for work. And this particular man had done just that. V.H. was working on his accounts early one morning when he glanced out the window and saw one of his men running toward the barn. V.H. suspected trouble. He decided to help by offering the man a safe place to stay. He opened the front door and called to him to come quickly inside. Without a second thought, V.H. showed the man up the stairs.

"Those are the same ones we just climbed," Brother explained.

He took him to . . .

Brother carefully placed the paper back in the suitcase and clicked it closed. "Come—let me show you." He stood up and then helped me with my chair, and we walked together into the hall. "Here, see this door?" Brother asked, pointing to a door in the wall.

Brother unlatched the door and slowly pulled it open, . . . "See? It's really a secret entrance to the attic."

"Yes." I said. "It looks just like our linen closet at home."

"But this one is a special linen closet. Remember when I told you the story about the tax collectors?" he said.

"Yes," I answered. "You mentioned that the Quakers didn't feel they should pay for the salary of the town minister because they didn't attend a town church, and that Quakers would sometimes hide their valuables in secret closets when the tax collector came."

"Well," said Brother "that's exactly what this is." Brother unlatched the door and slowly pulled it open, then stepped out of the way. "See? It's really a secret entrance to the attic."

"Wow!," I said. "How could anyone actually step that high into this closet? The door's at least three feet off the floor. You'd have to be a pretty tall person to be able to get in there. Or maybe use a stool or something to make the first step."

"You want me to lift you up so you can see?" he asked. "I have some friends who work here and I know they wouldn't mind."

I guess my eyes were as big as saucers, because Brother just gently lifted me up and I was standing at the foot of a short staircase that went straight up to what looked like the attic. "Go ahead," he said. "I'm right behind you."

I climbed a few steps and Brother had somehow managed the first step too. We climbed up together.

"This is so neat!" I exclaimed. "I love attics when there's someone else with me.

Hidden staircase at the Maine Maid Inn, where Anna and Brother had lunch and talked about Thomas Jackson's memoir of 1844 (Velsor Collection).

Look over there—I always wondered where restaurants stored their old furniture and holiday decorations."

"Come over this way," said Brother, as he pointed to a small loft tucked in under one of the gables in the roof. "I think this is where the escaping slave would have stayed. The story Thomas tells was that the fugitive was hidden all during that day and night, and then early next morning was taken by hay wagon to the next stop."

"Well, where did he go?" I asked. "Back to the Jackson Mill?"

"Oh, that's a good thought, but I don't think so. Jericho is only a few miles south of Long Island Sound, and Thomas writes that it wasn't safe to stay on Long Island because of the attitude toward escaping slaves," said Brother. "We can read some more after lunch and see what he said. I'm sure our lunch is ready—let's go back to our table and think about this for a minute."

Well, he had me then. Brother went down the stairs first. I don't think I was very graceful as we descended the stairs. Brother was waiting for me when I reached the last step, just in time for him to help me down.

A large plate of delicious French fries and a club sandwich with lettuce, tomato, turkey, and bacon greeted us. The sandwich was cut into quarters and so tall it had to be held together with toothpicks. I could hardly get it in my mouth.

"It all looks so wonderful, Brother. Thank you!"

"Thank you, Anna," Brother said with a large grin on his face. "I enjoy showing you all these things about my family, and about our town."

We ate our sandwiches quietly for a few minutes. We dipped our French fries in lots of ketchup and sipped the chilled lemonade.

"I think I'm in heaven," I said.

"Brother, where do you think Mr. Hicks took the escaping slave? Did he know someone the way Mr. Jackson knew the Seaman family? Was he related to somebody who would help?"

"That's an excellent question," Brother replied. He carefully wiped his hands on his frosty-white napkin and retrieved the memoir from the suitcase. "Thomas writes about that very thing right here."

V.H. asked me if I could help him bring a load of hay to the dock in the harbor the next morning. At the time, I didn't know what the load of hay really was. I said yes. When I arrived at his place I was surprised to

Hay wagon with false bottom, built in 1820-40 for hiding escaping slaves. At Valentine Hicks's request, Thomas drove such a wagon to the dock at the Roslyn Grist Mill (Mendenhall Plantation, Jamestown, NC; photograph, Velsor Collection).

see him hitching up the horses, and the hay already in the wagon. I apologized for being late, and he just smiled and thanked me for coming. When we reached the dock, S. M. met us with his sailboat. He took the "cargo" across the Sound to a relative in Westchester. That's the first time I helped an escaping slave to freedom.

"Wow, Brother. That's so wonderful! Thomas must have been amazed to find a slave hiding in the wagon. Does he mention other stories? Why do you think he was asked to help?"

"Well, I wondered about that also. I think that asking Thomas to drive the wagon made it look like a normal trip. Also I think, if I did my math right, that Thomas would have been in his sixties by then and he was no doubt a very hard-working, loyal man who had continued to live in Jericho and earned the respect of all who knew him. So, I guess you could say he was good cover. And yes, Thomas mentions some other stories. One I know you would like takes place just about the same time only a little east from here. Maybe you've heard of this family. My father's great-great-grandmother Sallie worked on the Willis farm and helped with the whitening of the linen. That's the story I was starting to tell you about before. Anyway, it's a real good one."

"This story is never-ending, Brother. And now you mention the Willis's. Do you think they were related to my father's family? I wonder, did they live here in Jericho?

"It's a good possibility, Anna. Why don't you ask your father when you go home tonight?" Brother said.

"I think that may be a good idea," I said. "These stories are really exciting, especially when you can see where they actually happened. I'll have to start another notebook just to keep up with your storytelling. Thanks for a wonderful lunch, Brother. You're just full of surprises!"

We each tucked a tiny leftover-treat into our pockets for Fox, and headed toward the stairway down—the stairway so full of secrets!

As we walked past the closet door, I smiled. I felt as if I knew a very special piece of history. How was I going to explain all this to my family? I had simply never realized that Brother felt he was different from me. Should I tell Mother? After all, our histories may be kind of the same at least for one or two stories. I'm sure that Fox and I will think of something before suppertime tonight.

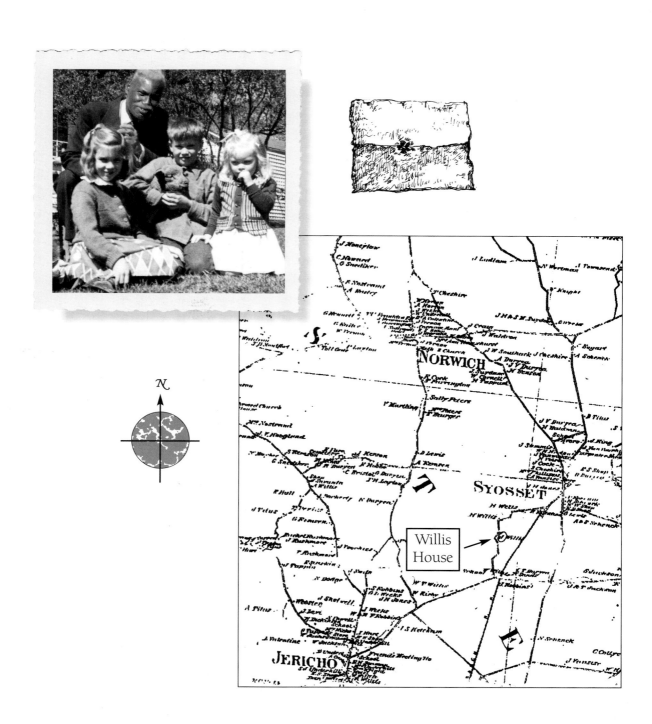

Willis
House

N

NORWICH

SYOSSET

JERICHO

August 17, 1955 – The Willis Family

 ummer days and early evenings are best spent outside doing things that parents definitely would not approve of. Like this afternoon, when my younger sister dared our brother to jump on the back of the vegetable truck as it passed by. Just seeing my brother run and jump onto the moving truck reminded me of Thomas and those other brave people who seized every moment to escape to freedom.

I had to laugh as I watched my brother frantically push big mounds of pea pods into the street, and jump back off the moving truck as my sister picked up the prized fresh vegetables from the road. There are just some things that have to be kept a secret from your family, otherwise it isn't any fun anymore. And that's when I decided to keep my story with Brother just for the two of us, at least for now.

And that's when I decided to keep my story with Brother just for the two of us, at least for now.

After I finished my final entry in the first notebook—completely filled already!—I decided to write Brother a thank-you note for taking Fox and me to lunch. I folded a white piece of paper and drew Elias's house on the front of the card. Inside I simply said:

> *Thanks for sharing your family with me.*
> *I have had a wonderful time.*
> *Love, Anna and Fox*

When Fox and I arrived at his house for our next Wednesday visit—the last before I went off to camp—Brother was waiting for us on the front porch. Lemonade and cookies were waiting for us too. Brother already had the old suitcase open and he was rustling through the papers inside it. I greeted him with a cheerful hello and handed my card to him. He smiled as he recognized Elias Hicks's house and read the note. He was silent for a moment.

"Thank you, Anna," he finally said. "You have made my family all the more important to me. Just thanks for listening. I'm glad we have today before you leave for camp."

"You're welcome, Brother," I said. "I love being a listener for you, and learning so much! Actually, I've come back to hear more about your father's great-great-grandmother Sallie and how she knew the Willis family. Do you suppose she ever knew *my* father's great-great-grandmother?" I asked cheerfully.

"I was just looking for the document that explains who the Willis's were. What was the name of your father's great-great-grandmother?" Brother asked.

"That's a good question," I replied. "I think her name began with an M. That's the initial stitched onto the sampler in our kitchen and I think she's the one who sewed it. I guess I have to ask my father that question. It never made any difference to me until you started telling your story." And then Brother just started in the way he always does.

"Here's the property called Locust Grove—just east of the Jericho Friends Meeting House near where we were last week," Brother said. "I remember finding

Map of Jericho and Syosset, 1859, showing the site of Anna Willis's house (Syosset Public Library Special Collection).

a copy of a map from 1859 and it showed all the properties. Here it is."

Brother pulled out a folded piece of paper with a hand-drawn map that must have been copied from an original—a really old one. The map showed Locust Grove—a large portion of property that Brother told me is still there between what is now Jericho and Syosset. The property seemed to extend from Kirby Lane all the way to where the railroad tracks are today. Everything was carefully labeled. There were three houses shown on the Willis farm just north of Jericho Turnpike.

"This is where it all took place," Brother said, pointing to the old map. "Thomas met his wife when he was delivering milk from the dairy farm to the Willis family. She was from The Brush." He unfolded Thomas's memoir sheets and searched for the right paragraph. "Here is the story."

> *I never thought I would marry. I had far exceeded my years for such things. But love has no boundaries. I was simply delivering milk for the young ones at the Willis farm when I was quite taken by a pretty young woman named Sallie. It was the summer of 1785. She had come to the farm to help with the linen whitening and with the children. Like me she had lived in The Brush. We seemed to have a lot to say to each other. Her mother's name was Harriet and her father's name was Jacob, and they all worked at Jackson's Mill too. Every morning when I came by she would greet me with a smile. Sometimes she would share some freshly baked bread and a few kind words. One thing just led to another. I met her parents and we were married that fall and I've been a married man ever since.*

Here it was! The connection between Brother's family and mine! I was sure of it. I decided to stay quiet about the connection for now—what exactly would it turn out to be? Did Brother already know?

I love the way Thomas uses his words, Brother." I said. "He sounds like such a character, doesn't he?"

"You're absolutely right," said Brother. "Sometimes he talks a great deal and then other times he doesn't say much. But look here, Anna. See the way he wrote this story, and then wrote another story in between the lines upside down?"

Brother pointed out the pattern for me to see. "This is where our next story begins. It seems that Sallie worked for the Willis family when a young boy came to stay with them in around 1829. Don't get confused here, because this Mr. Willis's name was Thomas also—and he was the son of Fry and Ann Seaman

Willis. I want you to remember the Seaman name for another story, so don't forget it—okay?" said Brother.

I nodded my head in response. I had a little idea where this was going but Brother was eager to tell his story so I didn't want to interrupt him. I just sipped my lemonade.

"It seems that after Thomas Jackson and Sallie were married, Sallie continued to help out at the Willis's whenever she could. During the summer of 1829, in August, Sallie was working at the Willis house one day when she met a nice young black man. His name was Henry. Of course, Thomas refers to him as a colored man but Negro people don't call themselves that anymore but that's a whole other story. Here's what Thomas writes."

Sallie described the young man as possessing eyes that were bright and unclouded. He had a massive forehead and a finely shaped head, which might have been chosen by an artist. He was striking in his appearance. He was well dressed. He was very well educated. When he spoke his words came from his soul.

Sallie spent many hours with him listening to his story. I've written what I remember here so that others may know. I'm not sure where he is today, but I think I remember reading about him in the newspaper called The Colored American. *I think this is the same boy. He was a special sort of person.*

Sallie . . . had heard my story, but it all seemed a lot more real coming from a boy who was so much younger than she was.

"Who was he, Brother?" I asked.

"He was a young man whose parents were fugitive slaves," said Brother. "It really is a wonderful story. It's about a man named Henry Highland Garnet—you probably haven't heard of him? . . ."

So I learned that Thomas Garret was a Quaker who lived in Delaware and helped escaping slaves to freedom. It seems he met Henry's family in 1824. They had traveled up to Delaware with other slaves who were once members of the Mandingo tribe, and were taken originally from the west coast of Africa to the state of Maryland in the early 1800s. Henry told Sallie they had escaped north from Maryland with other relatives and had slept in the woods and tidal swamps in order to make their way to freedom. Mr. Garret met them and gave them clothes and shelter. He then provided them safe passage as far as New Hope, Pennsylvania. Sallie had always been free; thanks to the Jacksons her parents had gained their freedom when they lived in The Brush, so she had never known much about these years of hiding. Thomas wrote:

Sallie was very surprised to hear how this poor young boy had had to escape from slavery. She had heard my story, but it all seemed a lot more real coming from a boy who was so much younger than she was.

How did this Henry end up on Long Island when they had gone to New Hope?" I asked. "For a group of people without cars and telephones, how did everyone know where to go and what was safe? It certainly took courage. How did Henry's family know what to do?"

"Well," Brother began. "It seems that Henry's father and mother felt they would be safer in bustling New York City than elsewhere, because slave catchers could come up from slave states to recapture their property. So the family had left New Hope for New York City later in 1824. Henry told Sallie that as soon as they reached the city his father had a kind of celebration. Here's what Thomas wrote about that."

Henry told Sallie that as soon as his family reached safety at last in New York City they had a simple ceremony that his father conducted at home. He proclaimed his family to be free. He gave thanks to God. He renamed everyone in the family. His mother was originally called Henny and he changed her name to Elizabeth, his sister was renamed Eliza, he was given the name of Henry, and his father renamed himself George. Their last name was to be Garnet in honor of Mr. Garret—they changed just one letter—who had helped them so much.

"Let me get this straight, Brother," I said, "Henry's family escaped from Maryland all the way to New York, but they still were not free?"

"Yes, Anna. That's the way it was. If a slave escaped to New York he could still be recaptured by his original slave owner—or else by a hired slave catcher who would take him back to his owners," said Brother.

"That doesn't seem fair!," I exclaimed to Brother. "So was Henry on the run when he came to the Willis farm?"

"Yes," said Brother. "Apparently Henry's father was a slave but knew the worth of education and encouraged young Henry to attend the African Free School in New York City, which he did from 1826 to 1828. And it's a good thing that he did. The schools were organized and run by a society known as the

Manumission Society, and its members would later save Henry's life."

"Oh, that's the word that you used before, manumit, right?" I said. "It means to set free. So this Society had schools for former slaves?" I asked.

"Well, something like that," answered Brother. "Actually the schools were created to educate these children so they would have a firm foundation in Christian values—and could find jobs and support themselves when they were older. The interesting part is that people from Jericho like Valentine Hicks were involved in this Society—probably from when he lived in the city. Henry loved the Manumission Society's school. He told Sallie that. Here it is:"

The happiest days of Henry's life were when he attended the African Free School on Mulberry Street. He had many good friends. His cousin James McCune Smith and Alexander Crummell were his best friends. He studied a lot but he had fun too. At thirteen he created a special club. The main purpose of the club was to not celebrate July the Fourth, the country's Independence Day, as long as slavery existed. Instead, on that day they would gather to plan ways for freeing and educating our race. The other thing they talked about was that after they were finished with school, they would go back to the South and help our brethren in bondage.

"Brother, how old was Henry when he came to Jericho and met Sallie at the Willis farm?" I asked.

"From what I can gather he would have been around fifteen years old."

"That's funny, I mean, he was just a few years older than Thomas when he escaped. Why exactly did Henry come to Jericho anyway," I asked. "Did he stay?"

"Evidently, as Sallie told Thomas, Henry had loved his school years, felt proud of them, and when he finished school he wanted to see a little of the world," said Brother. "He had taken a job on a cargo ship as a cabin boy in 1828. He made two voyages to Cuba. When he returned to New York City he returned to an empty home. His family was not there. His house was destroyed. He did manage to locate his family and learned of a terrible tragedy. Thomas wrote down the story that Henry told to Sallie . . . here. It's a little hard to read, upside down between the lines of other stories, but I'll give it a try:"

One evening during the summer a white man came to Henry's family's home in New York City. It turns out that the man was related to Colonel Spencer, their old master. Henry's father answered the knock at the door. The man asked if George Garnet lived there. Suddenly his father recognized the man's face from his master's, and wondered how he had discovered their family's new name. "Yes," he replied. The slave catcher did not recognize Henry's father. "Is he at home?" was the next question. "I'll go see," he said. Henry's mother and sister were in the room when his father passed into the side bedroom. He whispered hurried instructions to them, saying to stay there safely while he ran into hiding. The window was open and George jumped twenty feet to the ground, just missing the ill-tempered watchdog that lived in the yard. For some good-luck reason the dog never made a sound as Henry's father escaped down the alley to the street.

"That's an incredible story, Brother," I said. "Was George Garnet all right? What happened to Henry's sister and his mother?"

"According to Thomas, a friend who lived across the street and ran a grocery store took Henry's mother and sister into hiding until George could safely return. All of their household furniture was destroyed or stolen. The family was safe after all, but they were left with nothing and had to start their lives all over again," Brother said. I could hear the sadness in his voice.

"That's such an awful story, Brother," I said. "Is that why Henry came to Jericho? Because he had no place to go?"

"That's an incredible story, Brother," I said. "Was George Garnet all right? What happened to Henry's sister and his mother?"

"There's more," said Brother. "You see, after Henry found out that his family's home had been destroyed, he felt helpless, I guess, and decided to seek revenge. He took the money he had earned on the cargo ship and purchased a large clasp knife. With knife in hand, he marched down the center of Broadway with the intention of assaulting the slave hunter. His Quaker Friends saved him. They surrounded him, and that night he was brought secretly by wagon out to Long Island, to the home of Thomas Willis."

"Brother," I said. "How did his friends know to take him to Jericho?"

"That's the most important question, Anna," he said. "I think it had to do with the people who lived in Jericho in those years. You know that the early Quakers had come to Long Island sometimes directly from England, or sometimes from the other East Coast towns, so they could live their own lives freely— to their own religious and personal standards. And at the same time they had worked to end slavery fifty years before the State of New York's final law to end it took effect in 1827. Many of the Jericho and Westbury Quakers were members of the Manumission Society, and knew other people from New York and Westchester who were also members. So I think it was just a matter of taking Henry to a place they knew would be safe, and far away from the city.

But the story doesn't end here, Anna! Henry Garnet stayed with the Willis family for only about two weeks. He was then taken to Smithtown. Thomas writes about it."

> *Evidently, Henry went to Smithtown to the home of Captain Epenetus Smith, who indentured him for two years.*

"Do you know what it means to be indentured?"

"No," I said. Indentured. I thought about the word a moment as I sipped my lemonade.

Brother continued. " 'Indentured' means that someone binds himself to work as an apprentice for someone else for a period of time to learn a trade."

"I don't understand," I said. "Why would someone give up his freedom to be indentured to another person?"

Epenetus Smith's house in Smithtown, built in 1700 and 1750 on what is today Route 25A, where Henry Highland Garnet was apprenticed to Capt. Smith in 1829 (Velsor Collection).

"Anna, remember that Henry still wasn't officially free," Brother said. "I'm not sure but I think that being indentured was just a way of giving Henry a legal home in case he was ever found by a slave catcher."

"What happened next, Brother?" I asked. "Please tell me the rest before I have to go home!"

"Thomas writes here that he heard about Henry Garnet after he left Jericho," Brother responded. "We know Henry finished his two years of apprenticeship well, then went on to become a minister and fought for the freedom of all of his people. He became famous for his determined efforts. I think I have a copy of *The Liberator* in the suitcase. One of my relatives added that to the collection, maybe because it mentions Henry. Here, look at this paper, Anna. It's *The Liberator*, dated February 11, 1860. It is five columns wide with just print—no pictures. See here, on the bottom left hand column is a short ad."

The Rev. Henry Highland Garnet (1815-1882; Queens Historical Society Collection).

> *Shiloh Church—Rev. Henry Highland Garnet, pastor of Shiloh Presbyterian Church will preach on Sunday, the 12th inst, afternoon and evening. Subject in evening "The Prophetees." Rev. J. R. Rogers, one of the Kentucky exiles, will preach at 3 o'clock.*

"I guess you're right." I said. "We read that Henry did become a minister. That was after Thomas died, right? I mean Thomas was about ten in 1763, so when did he die? You said he died in 1844, the year of the memoir, so it must have been Sallie who put this in the suitcase, don't you think?"

You're right. I never gave that much thought," he said. "I think Sallie must have found this clipping and added it to the memoir. In fact it must have been Sallie, not Thomas, who wrote about hearing that Henry became a minister. That explains the different handwritings. I get my dates all mixed up. Thanks, Anna. You helped us get it all straight—it's hard going back and forth in time, and from place to place with different families. I'm glad you're writing it all down. . . .

"And you know, Anna, there are many other stories in the suitcase about escaped slaves coming to Jericho. All this time I thought Thomas had written them down. Maybe it was Sallie. I'll have to check the handwriting before our next meeting. And why don't you check on your relative whose name starts with an M—the one who stitched the sampler in your parents' kitchen?"

"Sounds like a good plan to me," I said. I placed my empty lemonade glass carefully on the wicker table before I stood to say good-bye. "Brother," I said, "I'm sure going to miss these meetings while I'm away at camp."

Brother just smiled his great smile and said, "So will I, child. So will I."

I didn't realize I'd been sitting on my foot for so long. As I got up I had a tingly feeling in my right leg. I couldn't help but laugh at myself. I guess I had sat so long in one position that I forgot what I was doing. Fox must have wondered why I was walking so strangely.

"Come on, Fox," I said as I kissed Brother good-bye. "You know, I go away to camp on Saturday and when I come back it will already be Labor Day weekend. I don't think I like school as much as Henry did," I said, as I waved good-bye. "I'd rather be over here talking with you! Well, see you in two weeks!"

As Fox and I made our way back down the street I noticed some small American flags hanging on a telephone pole. They must have been left over from the Fourth of July parade. I hadn't noticed them before. I couldn't help but think about Henry. How different our lives were. Here I am forgetting about the parade, never even noticing these flags, and there was Henry Garnet protesting the celebration of the Declaration of Independence because he was not free. "I guess his friends weren't free either, Fox," I said. "Do you have any idea how lucky we are—my brother and sister and me? I mean, all we have to do is be home for supper and poor Henry didn't even have a home to go to."

As Fox and I neared our house I could hear the voices of some children and their parents playing in our neighbor's yard. I could smell the sweet smell of hot dogs cooking on the grill. Sounded like a family picnic.

"Family! That's it, Fox!" I said. "I'll just happen to ask Mother! Of course she'll know who M.W. was, and I won't even bring attention to my project with Brother."

As I glanced up I saw my family driving home in our old gray Buick. "Here come Mother and Father," I said out loud. Fox lifted his head to the familiar sound of the car's engine as they made their way down the street. I felt better just knowing I wouldn't be going home to an empty house. What would I have done if I were Henry Garnet, I wondered. Funny, I couldn't come up with an answer.

August 18, 1955 – Who Is M.W.?

It was Thursday morning, just one day after my last amazing time with Brother. I was leaving for camp on Saturday and I really wanted to know about our family's sampler person M.W. before I left. I decided there was no easy way of approaching the subject without just coming out and asking. So that's just what I did. When I made my way quietly into the kitchen that morning, Mother was across the room stirring up some frozen orange juice.

I slipped into a chair at the table and said, "Mother, do you have any idea who this M.W. was who sewed our sampler?" She turned right around and gave me one of her great good-morning smiles, "Oh, hello, Anna. I didn't hear you come in. What did you say?"

I decided there was no easy way of approaching the subject without just coming out and asking. So that's just what I did.

"I was asking about the initials on the sampler that hangs over the table. It was signed by M.W. Who was that?" I asked.

"Oh, her name was Mary. But I'm not sure whether that was your great-great-grandfather Jacob's wife Mary, or their daughter Mary. Father's great-grandmother was Mary Kirby, I think, but I do get that side of the family mixed up. People all seem to have had similar names, and they tended to marry generations of people with the same last names," Mother said, waving her hands around as if giving up trying to make sense of my father's family.

"Wait a minute. Kirby?" I said. "That's a name of a street in Jericho. "Why would anyone be named after a street?"

Mother laughed and said, "Actually it's the other way around. They named the street after the family who lived there. But you're right. That's exactly where

Frederick Douglass (1817-1895) as a young man (Queens Historical Society Collection).

the family is from. They lived right near the big Willis farm. The Kirbys had four daughters. Amy was the most famous. Do you know who she was?"

"No." I said. But now I was really sorry I had started this conversation. Mother's a teacher, so sometimes she forgets we're not all in class. I drank my orange juice, hoping the discussion would end with the Amy Kirby question unanswered. Wrong! Mother poured a cup of coffee and sat down at the table.

"This much I do know," she said. "She, Amy, I mean, married Isaac Post from Westbury. It's a long story, but she moved to Rochester, New York, with her husband in 1828 and later worked with the famous abolitionist Frederick Douglass. They worked together—with many others—to end slavery. Actually they were part of the Underground Railroad. Do you know what that was?" Mother asked.

"Yes, I think I do." I said. "Do you think there was an Underground Railroad on Long Island? Do you think that's why Mary W. wrote those mysterious words on her sampler?"

Mother turned to look at the sampler hanging behind her on the wall. She seemed to be reading it for the first time. She read it aloud.

> *The runaway slave came to my house he stopt outside. He stayed with me a week before he recuperated and pass'd north.*

"Anna, I had actually forgotten what was written on this," Mother said. "I always look at the little cottage that Mary stitched here. It seems so charming. But that's a good question about the words, and the Underground Railroad on Long Island. I wonder who would ever know the answer to that?"

"Well, the little I know about the Underground Railroad is, that it was really pretty secret stuff. I mean, weren't people put in prison for helping slaves run away?" I asked.

"That's right, Anna, but there weren't any slaves on Long Island, so why

The mysterious sampler in Anna's kitchen.

would people help here?" Mother seemed to be mumbling her words, kind of talking to herself. For a teacher, she seemed to be at a loss. Didn't she know about slavery here? She stood and poured herself a second cup of coffee.

"Well, Mother," I said. "I really think there were slaves here on Long Island. In fact, Brother has told me some stories that are pretty amazing. He found the stories in some old papers that his family has handed down from generation to generation. Do we have anything like that in our house? I mean, besides the old Bible that shows everyone's name with their dates—the one that Father has in his office?"

"Well, let me think," Mother said. "There is an old blue suitcase in the attic. Your father brought it back when your grandmother died. Remember that one?"

"Yes, sure," I said. Things were suddenly looking up in our kitchen.

"I don't think I've ever opened that suitcase. Maybe today is the day."

"I'll get it," I offered. "Okay?"

As I ran up the stairs I was kicking myself for not talking to Mother much earlier. Sometimes parents aren't such a nuisance after all. Actually, maybe our old suitcase could help put some pieces together regarding Brother's old suitcase. Wouldn't that be something?

Actually, maybe our old suitcase could help put some pieces together regarding Brother's old suitcase. Wouldn't that be something?

"The attic," I said out loud. I always feel a little funny going into the attic. Why did I say I would do this by myself? The key is always left in the door with a ribbon tied through the keyhole. I'm not sure why. I think it's so you don't get locked in, and don't lose the key while you're inside looking for something. I opened the door, placed the ribbon around my neck, and climbed up the steep stairs. It was kind of stuffy up there. Kind of cobwebby, too, and dark. I quickly pulled the chain and turned on the light.

"This could take a while," I realized, as I glanced around the cluttered attic. Piles of boxes here, piles of boxes there. Where would the suitcase be?

I felt very much alone until I heard a soft jingle coming up the stairs behind me. I turned and saw Fox. "Nice to see you, Fox," I said. "I read somewhere that animals and ghosts don't mix. I hope that's true!"

"Well, I was going to keep this a secret," I told Fox. "But the minute I find the suitcase we're going right back to the nice safe kitchen."

Luckily, my search was soon rewarded. Hidden behind the Christmas decorations was a small blue cardboard-and-leather suitcase, faded with age. I moved a few boxes aside and picked it up. Without looking behind me I went right to the door, pulled the light chain, and carried the suitcase straight down the attic stairs. Fox beat me to the bottom.

"You're no better than I am, Fox! Spooky place, isn't it?" I locked the door and hurried the rest of the way down to show the suitcase to Mother.

By the time I got back to the kitchen Father was there too. He sat across from Mother at the table, drinking coffee and peacefully reading the morning paper. He looked up and saw both me and the blue suitcase at the same time.

"Good morning, Anna. I hear you're interested in finding out about your great-great-grandmother, Mary. And you've found the blue suitcase. Why the sudden interest?"

"Well, all summer . . ." I began to answer, still out of breath from dashing down from the attic, "I've been talking to Brother about his family and how they came to live on Long Island. And he found all this information in his father's great-great-grandfather's memoir from 1844 and I was just wondering if we had anything that we could read—like a diary or old letters or something that might tell us a little more about M.W. I mean—who she was, what she was like. . . ." I paused to take a breath.

Father smiled and seemed to welcome all my questions. Mother too—maybe this really was the right time to talk about my project with Brother. Maybe they really could help!

"Well, that blue suitcase is a good place to start." Father said. "I have trouble remembering the whole story and confess it's been a long time since I looked into that suitcase myself. Good luck in your detective work!"

"Well, it sounds as if I have my day's activities lined up," I said. "Thanks, Father." I was excited at whatever I was about to find out, and glad at last to have my family in on it.

I pushed the breakfast dishes to the side and placed the little blue suitcase on the table. I noticed that one of the latches was already open, so I quickly snapped the other latch free and lifted the top up on the case. Nothing seemed in any kind of order. I carefully picked through things and found an interesting old photograph—on the back it said who it was: it was my father when he was a boy.

Funny, he was wearing shorts and high socks and his hair was cut like a little Dutch boy's!

"How old were you, Father, when this picture was taken?" I asked.

Father put down the morning paper, lowered his glasses, and looked at the old photograph in my hand. "Oh, I don't know. Perhaps six or seven, I guess," he said. "My mother made me sit for that picture. I look pretty cute, don't you think?" He gave me a conspiratorial wink. "What else is in there?"

"Oh, mostly photographs. Looks like relatives, maybe at a picnic. Here you are all dressed up and outside," I said, holding the pictures up for Father to see. "And here are some letters, tied up in a blue satin ribbon. But there aren't any envelopes—the address is just written on the outside, and they're folded the way we do in school when we pass notes around the classroom. See what I mean?" I asked, holding them above the suitcase so Father could see.

"My, they look old," Father said. "I don't remember those being in there. Let me see?"

I handed the letters to Father, who was sitting on the other side of the table. He reached for them and put the paper down. He flipped through them and pulled one from the middle of the pile. "Oh, I see what you mean. This letter is dated 1838, May 7, from Amy Post, Rochester, to Mary Kirby, Locust Grove. Here's another one, also from Amy. You know, Anna," Father said, "you're related to Amy Post. Did I ever tell you that?"

"Mother just did." I replied. "I guess I need to find out more about her. Mother said she was involved in the Underground Railroad in Rochester. Do you suppose she's writing to Mary about that?" I asked.

"I don't think so," Father said. "People were afraid of being caught, so I don't think she would just write openly about it. But you never know. Would you like to read the letters?"

"I could give it a try, I guess," I said. I spoke calmly, but I was pretty excited, wondering what I might find.

Father handed me the letters, looked at his watch, and rolled his eyes. "Well, let me know, Sport. Time to go off to work, and we'll be wondering all day what you'll find."

There's that "good sport" name again. Guess I am one after all—all this investigating and stuff. Anyway, I was now in possession of some old family letters and extremely eager to read them. And at last, no more secrets from Mother and Father. I closed the suitcase and headed back upstairs to the comfort of my room. I was in for an amazing morning of discoveries . . . the time flew by.

Mother called up the stairs to tell me lunch was ready. I had read all about Mrs. Seaman's horrible affliction (not sure what it was!), the funeral of a young girl, a drought that hurt the farm crops, but nothing about slaves.

"No luck yet!" I said as I entered the kitchen.

Mother turned and smiled. "I've been waiting for you to come running down the stairs all morning," she said. "I guess I'm not surprised."

Mother continued, "Oh, I saw Brother the other day and I asked him about your lunch and he said he enjoyed your meetings on Wednesdays, talking about his family. You'll really miss him when you go to camp, don't you think? I know he'll miss the talks with you."

"I know. I feel funny about leaving Brother. I thought maybe I could find something in these letters before I left, but I can't seem to find anything at all. I guess I'm too excited about going to camp. I can't seem to concentrate."

"Would you like to take those letters over to Brother today? So he can read them while you're gone?" asked mother.

"I certainly would like to—that's a great idea! Thanks, Mother. Do you really think he'd like to read them?"

> *"I wonder if she knows something about these letters," I said to Fox as we walked up Clay Street later that afternoon to see if Brother was home.*

Mother laughed. "Yes, I do! I think this is just the thing to keep Brother intrigued while you're away at camp."

I thought about all this. The idea of taking the letters to Brother. Mother has this amazing habit of knowing things and not telling you, so you think you're in charge—like the letters. Had she been thinking about them all summer and just not telling?

"I wonder if she knows something about these letters," I said to Fox as we walked up Clay Street later that afternoon to see if Brother was home. The letters were safely tied up in my old blue-and-white bandana—held carefully in my hand. The sun was just starting to break through clouds, clearing after a gray beginning. As we walked I could hear the first autumn leaves crunching under the soles of my sneakers—that end-of-summer sound. The change from summer to almost-school is always dramatic to me. I realized I'm not one to like change, especially when change means not being able to see my friend Brother every Wednesday afternoon. And school means homework for all three of us and for me dance class and Girl Scouts and all those things that go with school. But first, before all that, I get to go to camp. I'm pretty excited about that! I hope Brother will understand.

As Fox and I walked across his lawn we found Brother with a basket of fresh zucchinis, just home from work and enjoying his garden. "Good afternoon, Anna. Hi, old friend!" he said as he shook hands with Fox. "I didn't expect to see you today. But while you're here, do you think your family would like some of these? The summer has been perfect for growing. I'll never be able to eat them all."

"Sure," I said. "Mother loves to make zucchini bread. And I actually like them stuffed. How about you?"

"Oh, I have stuffed them, baked them, stewed them and now it's time to share them," Brother said, as he handed me two huge zucchinis.

"My father's great-grandfather never saw the upstairs, but the story goes that there's a small room next to the chimney . . ."

"These weigh a ton, Brother. How long did it take to grow them?"

"Well, not very long," he replied. "That's the problem. Once they start growing there's no stopping them. I remember when I was just a boy, there were farms all around here—as far as you could see. In fact when my grandfather was around he would tell us about how the farmers had so many vegetables they took them into New York City to sell at the market."

Brother made his way up to the porch. And then he just started the way he always did, even though it wasn't Wednesday and our visit was a surprise.

"Anna, you know Sallie had a son and he was my father's great-grandfather. Well, here's one more story before you go off to camp. I just remembered it.

"When my father's great-grandfather was young he worked on a farm over here in Westbury. He loved to shear the wool off the sheep in the spring—but that's not the point of this story. It seems that these farmers would take their vegetables by wagon into New York. And this particular farmer was Joseph Hicks. His wife was Lydia Hicks and her grandfather was Isaac Hicks and her great uncle was Valentine

Hicks. Remember the man who used to live in what's now the Maine Maid Inn?"

"Wait a minute, Brother!" Anna exclaimed. "Do you mean Lydia Hicks married Joseph Hicks? Not another family marriage!"

"Well, in a way, yes—but they were only distant cousins. Joseph Hicks's farm was one of the first in Westbury—it was built before 1700 and I guess that's why my father's great-grandfather called it "The Old Place." Maybe you know the house. It's still there today on Post Road, close to the road. It's all white, and it's really two houses side by side. One is

The Seaman-Hicks House, built in 1695 and among the first in Westbury, was thus called "The Old Place." It still stands on Post Road in Old Westbury. Escaping slaves received shelter in the attic en route to the Roslyn Grist Mill and safety across the Sound (Richard Gachot Collection).

much older than the other. Nothing fancy about it, except it has a porch that stretches the full length of the house. The house itself is two stories and it faces south, so when you look at it from Post Road all you really see is the side of it.

"Anyway, Joseph Hicks and his family were farmers and they would regularly take their vegetables to the city to sell. The story goes that sometimes when things were safe, my father's great-grandfather would bring back fugitive slaves in Joseph Hicks's hay wagon, filled with city goods just the way it was for Thomas, remember? The wagon would usually get back home at night when the children were already in bed. The escaping slaves were fed and then taken to the attic of Joseph Hicks's farmhouse. My father's great-grandfather never saw the upstairs, but the story goes that there's a small room next to the chimney in the attic where they could spend the rest of the night. They stayed up there all day and when it was dark again the hay wagon would take them to the old mill in Roslyn for the trip across Long Island Sound. Of course, the problem was the tides at the mill. Have

The Roslyn Grist Mill, at the edge of Roslyn Harbor, was apparently once owned by the Seaman family. It is believed to have been a departure place for escaping slaves for trips across the Sound and points north—or to eastern Long Island—to safety (John Butler).

you ever been out there? The boats can't get close at low tide."

Well, here I was just dropping off some letters, and about to go off to camp, and Brother's telling me another amazing story! I was pretty sure I knew the mill he meant.

"Are you talking about the mill right in the middle of town?" I asked. "We went there on a field trip last year from school. No one mentioned it had anything to do with the Underground Railroad."

"Well, I'm not surprised," Brother said. "I guess that's just one more reason to write these stories down—so we don't all lose our history."

At that, Brother went inside to get the old brown suitcase, and balanced it on his knees while he carefully opened it one more time. This time he pulled out something I hadn't seen before—some typewritten sheets of paper—and ran his finger down the side margin as he looked for the sentence he wanted.

"This story was told by Henry Hicks, who was descended from Joseph Hicks," he said. Henry is the man who gave the speech in 1941.

"Was Henry related to Elias Hicks of Jericho?" I asked.

"Yes and no," said Brother. How many times had he said that—"yes and no!" It was surely getting complicated, all these interconnected families, and all those times Thomas Jackson was almost free but not quite. No wonder we needed to write things down.

Brother continued, explaining that they all seemed to be distant cousins, and yes, families are confusing. Then he read to me from Henry Hicks's story about his family several generations ago. "I like this one," he began.

> *In the morning the family dressed the male slave in their grandmother's clothes and took him to the dock where they were met by a friend who took him across the Sound.*

I was astounded. "Brother, why did they dress him up as a woman?" As I said that, I realized the answer to my own question. "I know! They wanted to hide his identity, right?"

"Yes," said Brother. "So people wouldn't be able to remember who they saw on the wagon. Children were disguised like that too."

"That's amazing, Brother," I said. "Where did you find out about that?"

"Oh, just about fifteen years ago when Henry Hicks made that speech—it was at the African Methodist Episcopal Church in Westbury. Well, he talked about old times in the town and about how his family were among the early Quaker settlers. He talked about the Hicks Nursery getting started in 1853, of course, but he told some old family stories of how they helped escaping slaves to freedom even before then."

It was surely getting complicated, all these interconnected families, and all those times Thomas Jackson was almost free but not quite. No wonder we needed to write things down.

Brother was thoughtful as he spoke. Big thoughts here, for both of us. Then he went on.

"The funny part was, Anna, that I had never heard stories like that before. I asked for a copy of his speech, and since Mr. Hicks had made up some for members of the church, I was given one by a friend. That's when I started to wonder about my own past. I began to look around my family's things, and that's when I came across this old suitcase—which I've been thinking about all these years. And then, you and I began our Wednesdays, and you're wondering about things too. How about you—did you find anything about M.W.?"

"I thought you forgot," I said. I reached over and carefully picked up my blue-and-white bandana, opening it to reveal my collection of letters tied in their faded ribbon. "I've been trying to read them all morning but I haven't found anything, and they're really hard to read—lines every which way, and all different sizes. I thought you might see something I missed."

I handed Brother the collection and watched him as his old hands gracefully undid the blue satin tie. "These all have different dates on them," he said. "Here's one from the 1820s—I can't make out the exact date, but it's to Mary W. at Locust Grove and it's from Rochester. Okay if I read this one first?" Brother asked. "Then the others, while you're off at camp?"

"Sure. Be my guest," I said. "I hope you find something good!"

"Well, you never know. I sure will try," said Brother. He spoke slowly, and I could tell he was thinking we wouldn't see each other for a while.

As Fox and I stood to say good-bye, I was thinking about that too. I love camp but right then I was really sorry I was leaving. Our Wednesday times together had come to mean so much to me.

"Maybe you can break the handwriting code, Brother. My eyes need a rest!" I said. "Hey!" I yelled to Fox. "Wait for me!" Fox had just zoomed off across the lawn.

Brother laughed out loud. "Fox has been watching that cat all afternoon, Anna. I guess he wasn't going to stand for it any longer."

With that, Brother tapped me on the shoulder. "Anna, I never was lucky enough to go to camp but I imagine it's great fun. Have the time of your life. We'll meet again when you come home."

I knew at that moment that somehow Brother was going to beat me at my quest to uncover the story behind my relative Mary W. Which was okay. After all, there really wasn't a story without Brother, now, was there?

"Thanks, Brother," I said. "Enjoy the read."

I just couldn't stop smiling. Now I had given Brother something after all, when he had already given me so much. And as for Fox, he was coming back up the street to meet me with his own smile of satisfaction matched by the lazy wagging of his furry collie tail. I guess the cat went home just the way we were about to do.

• • •

September 4, 1955 – Sunday

ast night Mrs. Green called and set the house astir—complaining that Fox had chased her prized cat Fluffy up her apple tree—and Father had to go over to her house and get the cat out of the tree. I guess Fluffy's fine because there haven't been any more calls. At that thought the telephone rang.

"Hello, Willis residence," I said.

"Hello, Anna. Welcome home!"

"Brother!" I said. "How are you? Are you at the Sweet Shop? I just got back yesterday from camp. I had the most amazing time! Did you get my postcard? I met some old friends from last summer and we shared lots of things. I told them all about you and our project. Did you enjoy the old Mary Kirby letters?"

"Brother!" I said. "How are you? Are you at the Sweet Shop? I just got back yesterday from camp. . . ."

"Yes, as a matter of fact I did, Anna. I just wanted to call and tell you I found something that will make you happy. Last night, I was rereading the letter you showed me—the very first one, remember? Well, just at the end of the letter on the back side, way up in one of the corners, was a small note. I would love to show it to you. I'll be home at three o'clock if you can wait till then."

"You're right," I said. "I don't know if I can wait but I'll sure try. Three o'clock at your house. We'll be there with bells on!" As I hung up the telephone I checked and it was only eleven o'clock. "It's going to be a long day, Fox," I said. "A long day."

I thought that if I helped wash the lunch dishes time would go by faster, but of course it didn't. So I took out the old blue suitcase and decided to see just what else was in there. I took out the old photographs, and underneath I found an old diagram of family names. It seems that Jacob Kirby Jr. married Mary Seaman and they had eight children. Three were girls—Mary, Hannah, and Amy Kirby. Mary Kirby of the letters! This was a good start. The family tree also showed that Hannah married Isaac Post, and then after her death Isaac married Amy. I guess he liked the Kirbys. But still no Mary Willis.

The clock in the kitchen must be broken, I thought. The hands just don't seem to be moving—it's not much past one o'clock.

At that moment Mother came into the kitchen. I told her about Brother's call and she could easily sense my impatience.

"You know, Anna, if you're looking for something to do you could clean out your dresser. It's that time of year. You could sort out all those things you've grown out of, and we need to start thinking about going back to school."

I wasn't sure what was worse: school, cleaning out my dresser, or just watching the hand of the clock not move.

"Mother, do you think if I cleaned all that stuff out of the drawers, that they'd actually close?" I asked.

"You know I can't remember ever seeing that dresser with the drawers all completely closed," said Mother.

"You know I can't remember ever seeing that dresser with the drawers all completely closed," said Mother. "In fact, when your Father and I were first married we used that dresser too. Your Father loved it so. He said it was from the original Willis farm. I always said it doesn't work right, but that didn't seem to bother him much. But you could try to make it work, why not?"

"I'll accept the challenge," I said. "But since I'm going to meet Brother at three o'clock, could you please call me at two-thirty? I don't want to be late. He said he found something of interest in one of Mary Kirby's letters."

"Oh, wonderful!" said Mother. "I'll keep my eye on the time."

Sorting clothes has to be the worst job. I always seem to forget which pile is the save pile and which is the give-away pile. And the whole time you have to remember that you are actually getting older, and that means more school work and family chores, but I guess it means birthdays and being able to do more things by yourself, too, like my older brother, who is allowed to just go anywhere it seems.

Well, the bottom drawer was finished at last. Keep this, give that away, all done.

I sat on the floor close to the bureau and pushed the drawer back in with both feet. As I pushed, I thought I saw what the problem was. One side moved faster than the other. Maybe soap would help—I'd just slide the soap back and forth along the runners beneath the drawer to make it slide smoothly. Then I'd do the bottom edges of the drawer itself. I'd seen Father do this once downstairs. Soap sliding against soap—brilliant! I took the bar of soap from the bathroom and got to work.

I emptied the drawer and put all the saved clothes in neat piles on the floor. This is taking longer than I planned, I thought. Oh, well.

I pulled the empty drawer all the way out of the dresser and put it off to one side. It sure was heavy. I took the soap and rubbed it inside along the bottom on the right. So now my dresser smelled like Ivory soap!

Next I started on the left side. Funny how dusty it is way back inside a dresser. As I ran the soap from front to back on the left, I couldn't get it to move smoothly. I reached back to see what was stopping the soap. My hand touched something really dusty. Where is Fox when I need him? I thought to myself.

"Fox, are you here? I mean just in case this was alive once?" Actually, Fox was right there behind me. He lifted his ears and stood up as if he knew he was called to duty.

"Thanks, Fox," I said. "You see that thing in the back of my dresser? Over there." I pointed to the dark dusty form on the runner way back inside the dresser. Fox looked but was not interested. I figured that was a sign it wasn't alive—now or ever. With that assurance I reached in and grabbed hold of it. It was crinkly, not soft—another good sign.

I pulled it slowly all the way out. In the daylight, I could see it was a folded piece of brown paper. It looked really old—all brown and fragile. I looked long and hard to make sure I remembered how it was originally folded. I felt my hands shaking. What had I found?

Slowly I opened one side and then the next and the next. There was a small tear in the center and I was especially careful with that. I stood up and went over to the window to get a better view. The ink was very pale brown, and difficult to read. I could barely make out the handwriting. Finally I could read it—

I Elias Hicks of the State of New York in Queens County and in the Township of Oysterbay have and do sett free from bondage or Slavery my Negro boy named Thomas Jackson and do hearby release . . .

What is this? I was sure I was dreaming. "Fox?" I called. His ears perked up again. Yes, I was awake.

"Mother?" I yelled. I jumped over the piles of clothes and raced down the stairs holding tight to my newly found treasure. "Mother! Mother!" I shouted.

"Yes, Anna," Mother paused and said. "Oh dear, I'm sorry. It's two-forty-five. You were so quiet I forgot to call you."

"Mother, look! Look! Do you know what this is?" I said, totally out of breath. "I think it's a manumission paper for Thomas Jackson. Oh, that's right, you don't know the story. Well, it's a long one. But the short one is that this could be Brother's father's great-great-grandfather's manumission paper. All this time it's been hiding in the bottom draw of our old dresser that's left over from the Willis farm. How did it get there? I can't wait to show it to Brother! I'll explain all this later."

I tucked the crinkly old paper safely into an envelope and kissed Mother and yelled to Fox, "Let's go!"

I can't remember how fast I ran. But it wasn't until I was well past the Ellis's house that I realized it was raining. Luckily the paper was safe in its envelope. As I skipped over the puddles it became very clear to me: Thomas Jackson must have lived with the Willis family after he married Sallie, and this must have been their dresser.

"Brother!" I yelled. "Guess what I found? There really is a story for both of us!"

I had never had the opportunity of stepping inside Brother's home because we were always in the wicker chairs on the porch. But this time with the rain he simply opened the door and said hello and in I went. I really was too excited! Fox shook himself off and followed me in.

I looked around. Wow. I was overwhelmed by his collection of antiques and by the feeling of comfort I felt as he hung up his coat and dried Fox off with a red and white dish towel. I waited as long as I could and then I just started the way he always does.

"Brother, I love your house. And I think you and I have a lot in common! You see, we have some really old furniture in our house too. In fact there is this dresser that I really never liked until today. It's really old and the drawers never close right. And today Mother made me clean out some clothes that just don't fit me anymore and when I did that I pulled out the bottom drawer and found this old piece of paper folded up and wedged into the back underneath the drawer on the left-hand side." I opened the envelope and handed the crinkly paper to Brother folded in exactly the same manner in which I found it. I watched his eyes to see his response.

Brother took the paper and just looked at it. "Anna, this is really old. What is it?" he asked.

"Go ahead. Look for yourself," I said. I never let on what I already knew.

Brother unfolded the paper carefully. It was difficult to read so he took it over to a lamp and held the paper under the light to get a better look. I could see his hands shaking, as he stood perfectly still reading the paper.

It seemed to take forever as Brother slowly read through the document— once, then again. He reached into his pocket for his handkerchief. I could see then for the first time large pools of tears forming in his dark brown eyes. He removed his glasses, wiped his eyes, and very quietly asked, "Where did you say you found this, Anna?"

"Brother!" I yelled. "Guess what I found? There really is a story for both of us!"

"I found it way in the back of my dresser," I said. "I have no idea how long it's been there. Mother told me the dresser used to belong to Father when he was a boy and lived on the old Willis farm, and that she didn't like it because the drawers would never close tight. I guess I found out why!"

"You certainly did," said Brother. He was very quiet. I wondered just what he felt about our shared discovery.

"So let me think," he finally said. "Does this really mean that Thomas lived with the Willis Family? All this time I thought Thomas lived on the dairy farm in Jericho where he worked. I guess that wasn't so. Well, this means that our families have been together for a very long time, Anna." He said it very softly, and was quiet for a moment.

Then he said, "And there's even more, Anna. Here, have a seat over here by the fireplace. Let me show you this letter of yours that Mary W. wrote in 1838. I guess she just never sent it to Amy, because here it is still in your packet of letters."

Brother left the room and came back with his old brown suitcase and Grandmother Willis's collection of old letters. "Let me find this. Now, I left it right on top so I could find it when you came. Here it is. I have no idea why Mary never mailed this, unless she was waiting to write again so she could fill up the page, and then somehow misplaced the letter. Folks had to be very frugal back then as you know. But I'm glad for our sake that she didn't mail it, because we might never have known the story if she had."

Carefully, Brother opened the letter signed M.W. and unfolded the last page and read it to me.

> *We have a young Negro girl staying with us. She is very well dressed and she can read and is very pretty. Cousin Sammy sent for her and Thomas brought her here from Flushing. I don't know how long she will stay.*

"So, who is Cousin Sammy?" Brother asked.

"I don't know who Cousin Sammy is," I said. "But Brother! This could be the same M.W. who cross-stitched our sampler! The one dated 1850 about the runaway slave! I think it's time to find out about all this. We're getting much closer. Father would know, and if he doesn't then we have the family Bible in the den and that's filled with names and birth dates. I don't know about you, but I just can't wait another week to find the answer." Brother smiled and started toward the closet to get his umbrella. "Let's take the car, Anna," he said. "The weather seems to be getting worse."

"Gladly," I said, remembering the drenching I'd had coming over. "Come on, Fox. Let's go for a ride."

I could see Mother's face through the window over the sink in the kitchen. She had a smile on her face when she saw I was bringing Brother to our house. I saw her stop her task and wipe her hands on her apron.

"Hello, what brings the research group to our house?" she asked, as she opened the door.

"Well, it seems that . . ." I began. "No, you go ahead, Brother. I don't want to rush your story."

Brother handed the letters to Mother and explained how he had read that Mary W. had a former slave staying with them whom someone named "Cousin Sammy" had sent for, and whom his great-great-grandfather Thomas Jackson had brought to Locust Grove from Flushing.

"Now we need to find out who Cousin Sammy was, Mother. Do you have any idea?" I asked.

Mother smiled a secret kind of smile and just said, "Follow me. There must be some information in the family Bible." We all marched into Father's den, a book-filled room just off the dining room, and sure enough Mother found the Bible wedged in between *Gulliver's Travels* and *Tom Sawyer*—two of my father's favorite books.

"Here it is!" she said, and placed it carefully on the desk. It was really old-looking and the binding was frayed all around. We opened the front cover and propped it up from beneath, and Mother started to read the names.

"Samuel Willis born 1704 married Mary Fry in 1728." she began.

"Mary Willis—M.W.!" I exclaimed. "But wait . . . that's much too early. Now I'm all confused again."

Mother kept reading.

"They had ten children: First Mary, John, Sarah, Jane, Amy, and Fry," Mother said as she began to read the names.

"Ten children!" I said. "That's a whole lot of children! Did they all survive?" I asked.

"I believe so," said Mother.

"No wonder we seem to be related to people all over the place. The Willis's had a good start," I said.

"But Brother! This could be the same M.W. who cross-stitched our sampler!"

Brother chuckled under his breath as I ranted on about our family, and Mother continued reading the family list.

"Here, Mary Willis was born in 1731 and married someone named Jackson from Jerusalem—maybe somehow connected to the Jacksons we know from Girl Scouts? That's present-day Wantagh. Right, Brother?" Mother asked.

Brother smiled in his quiet way. He didn't share his story about Wantagh and the community known as The Brush, at that moment—*or* his own family's long line of men named Thomas Jackson—but I knew. "Mother," I said. "What year was that?"

"I don't really know but it says that Mary Jackson had a daughter also named Mary," Mother said, pointing to the line written in the book.

"Who did *she* marry?" I said. "I'm completely confused by all of these Marys."

"She married William Seaman and moved to Jericho," Mother said.

"Oh, this is interesting," she continued. "And *their* daughter Mary Seaman married Jacob Kirby."

"Too many Marys, and too many husbands to keep track of!" I exclaimed.

"Well, at least this is where it seems to make some sense," Mother said. "*There's* your M.W., Anna!" Mother said. "Mary W. was really Mary W. Kirby, but because there were so many Marys she used the W., which probably stood for Willis, to identify herself."

"And that would explain why she was writing those letters to Amy Post in Rochester. Amy was her sister! And they were the great-granddaughters of Mary Willis, married into the Jackson family from Jerusalem."

A thought came to me. "Brother, whose house did Sallie do her work in?" I asked.

"Oh, that was Fry and Ann Willis," Brother responded. "They had a son named Thomas who would be around the same generation as Mary W.," Brother said. "Are they listed in this book?"

Mother ran her eyes down the long list of relatives. She paused, and pointed to a name. "Here, Fry is Mary Willis's younger brother. Yes, he married Ann Seaman in 1770 and they had two sons, Thomas and Isaac. Their youngest sister, here it is. Oh, Anna—we found it! Look, Brother, here. Mary and Fry's sister was Jane Willis. And she married James Parsons. Jane was his second wife—they were married in 1780. Jane became the stepmother to John, James, and Sammy Parsons. Isn't that the story you came home with? So, Mary W. Kirby's stepcousin was Sammy Parsons. Does that help your story, Brother?"

Just as we were all reflecting on that thought, Mother started to pick up the Bible with one hand, and something fell out on the desk.

"Yes, it surely does," Brother said. "It seems our families were always neighbors and always helping each other."

Just as we were all reflecting on that thought, Mother started to pick up the Bible with one hand, and something fell out on the desk.

"What's this?" I asked. "It looks like a piece of newspaper."

I unfolded the old paper and found a long article about someone named Samuel Bowne Parsons. I couldn't read the date. I started to read the words. It seemed to be about the Parsons family from Flushing. Someone had underlined a paragraph that said:

> His stepmother was Jane Willis from Locust Grove. He has been remembered as a religious man who helped more slaves to freedom than any other man in Flushing.

"I wonder if Father knows this story," I asked. "What do you think, Mother?"

Just then Father pulled into the driveway. I was so excited about the day's events that I ran to the screen door to tell Father to come and read the article we'd just found in the family Bible. Fox met him in the driveway and danced circles of excitement around the car, and then around Father too.

Father put his briefcase down in the drive and gave Fox a big hug. I wanted to tell Father everything about our summer's research discoveries right then. But I didn't. I just asked him to come into the den and meet Brother, who was studying the family Bible. Father just gave me a funny look and I followed him into the house.

"Hello, Brother," he said. "Welcome! Anna, did you two ever find out who Mary W. was?"

"Yes, I think we did," I said. "And we found out a whole lot more, too!"

"Come, let's sit down and have some lemonade," said Mother. "I think the researchers have a great many stories to tell us."

I didn't tell Brother's story because that is his. But I did tell Father about the manumission paper in my dresser, and the relatives from so long ago listed in the Bible and that I knew who "M.W." was at last. Mary Willis Kirby, the stitcher of our sampler and the source of the mysterious verse.

And then Brother told his family stories over dinner that night. It was a long, wonderful dinner that none of us will ever forget—not Mother, not Father, not Brother, not my brother and sister, and definitely not me!

After the dishes were done Fox and I walked Brother to his car. The rain had stopped and the night was clear, kind of like our old family stories, at last. I had never felt so close to Brother before. I took his hand. I could feel that his hand was much larger than mine. It was strong and gentle at the same time.

"I love you, Brother." I said.

"I love you too, child. Sweet, sweet, child. I love you, too."

I gave Brother a big hug. And Fox wagged his tail as Brother shook his paw good-bye. . . .

I knew at that moment that somehow Brother was going to beat me at my quest to uncover the story behind my relative Mary W. Which was okay. After all, there really wasn't a story without Brother, now, was there?

I emptied the drawer and put all the saved clothes in neat piles on the floor. This is taking longer than I planned, I thought. Oh, well.
I pulled the empty drawer all the way out of the dresser and put it off to one side. It sure was heavy. I took the soap and rubbed it inside along the bottom on the right. So now my dresser smelled like Ivory soap!
Next I started on the left side. Funny how dusty it is way back inside a dresser. As I ran the soap from front to back on the left, I couldn't get it to move smoothly. I reached back to see what was stopping the soap. My hand touched something really dusty. Where is Fox when I need him? I thought to myself.
"Fox, are you here? I mean just in case this was alive once?"
Actually, Fox was right there behind me. He lifted his ears and stood up as if he knew he was called to duty.
"Thanks, Fox," I said. "You see that thing in the back of my dresser? Over there." I pointed to the dark dusty form on the runner way back inside the dresser. Fox looked but was not interested. I figured that was a sign it wasn't alive—now or ever. With that assurance I reached in and grabbed hold of it. It was crinkly, not soft—another good sign.
I pulled it slowly all the way out. In the daylight, I could see it was a folded piece of brown paper. It looked really old—all brown and fragile.
I looked long and hard to make sure I remembered how it was originally folded. I felt my hands shaking. What had I found?

September 22, 1955 – Back to School

ell, it's definitely school time again, and it's okay after all. Books, teachers, homework, friends—same as always. But things have changed in lots of good ways. Mother has invited Brother to school to speak about his family history. And I have it all written down in my two Notebooks—the story of Thomas Jackson and Sallie, Elias Hicks, and our families from so many generations ago.

I have seen Brother in town a few times, and I can see we both miss our Wednesday meetings. But Mother said that our family would all be together this year at Thanksgiving and that includes Brother Jackson and me.

Brother's Lemonade

For each cup of water, add:
1 1/2 tablespoons of fresh squeezed
  lemon juice
3 to 4 tablespoons sugar
1/8 teaspoon of salt

The sugar and water need not be boiled, but the quality of the lemonade is improved if they are. Boil sugar and water 2 minutes. Chill syrup and add lemon juice. Add water, fresh sliced lemons. Add 1 tray ice cubes and 2 cups water; stir until cold.

Brother's Oatmeal Cookies

Makes about 3 dozen cookies
Preheat oven to 350 degrees

Ingredients:
1/2 cup brown sugar
1/2 cup white sugar
1/2 cup butter
1 cup flour
1/2 teaspoon soda
1/2 teaspoon double-acting
  baking powder

Measure:
1/2 cup brown sugar, firmly packed
1/2 cup granulated sugar

Cream with:
1/2 cup of butter

Combine and beat in until smooth:
1 egg
1 teaspoon vanilla
1 tablespoon milk

Sift together and add to the above ingredients:
1 cup all purpose flour
1/2 teaspoon soda
1/2 teaspoon double acting baking soda
1/2 teaspoon salt
1/2 teaspoon cinnamon

When beaten smooth add:
1 cup uncooked quick rolled oats
1 cup raisins or chocolate chips
1 teaspoon grated orange rind
  Beat mixture well. Drop cookies by teaspoonfuls 2 inches apart on well-greased cookie sheet and bake until light brown.

Author's Note –
Historical Fiction Based in Fact

The story of Anna Willis and Brother Jackson and his forebear Thomas Jackson is essentially fiction; they are alive only in the minds of those who can understand the need to search for one's identity. Yet their friendship is real and their story is important to our understandings of American history, and while the story is fictional it is based in fact.

The lives of Anna and her family are in many ways just like those of real people who lived in Westbury in the 1950s, and the Willis farm did exist in Locust Grove— just east of Jericho between Kirby Lane and Underhill Boulevard. The Jericho Meeting House, the Maine Maid Inn, and Elias Hicks's home are still standing on "Old Jericho Turnpike" in Jericho and are part of today's Jericho Historic Preserve. The Westbury Meeting House still stands in Westbury, the third on its site, on the corner of Jericho Turnpike and Post Avenue.

Among the historical facts on which *Brother & Me* is based are these:

★ Brother Jackson and his family and each of his ancestors are drawn from history. Sallie represents an actual person who came to Jericho in 1830 from The Brush to work at the Willis family farm. Thomas Jackson's escape as recounted in the 1763 *Gazette* is from an actual newspaper clipping, and the italicized memoir extracts are derived from the clipping. Henry Highland Garnet as well as other escaping slaves did hide at the Willis farm on a number of occasions until they could be taken to safety.

RUNAWAY

On the 30th of January 1778, a negro boy named Alick, about fifteen years of age. Had on when he went away: a check shirt, reddish coloured jacket, breeches, stockings and hat. He is branded on the breast with the letters **R.W.**

Whoever will secure said boy, or give information of any person or persons harbouring him, shall receive Four Dollars reward from **Richard Wright** in George Street, No. 22.

All Masters of Vessels are forbid harbouring, or carrying off the said boy on their peril.

★ Slavery did exist for some time on Long Island as elsewhere in the colonies and in the country. According to the 1771 census there were 2,236 Negroes, most of whom were enslaved, in Queens County (which includes today's Nassau County) on Long Island. This meant that 1 out of every 5 people was enslaved.

★ "The Brush" was an actual destination for escaping slaves to hide and to live in. The Brush was located in the Twin Lakes preserve in present-day Wantagh. There is an African American Burial Ground located on Oakfield Avenue in North Bellmore, New

continued

York, the property for which was donated by Thomas Jackson—a direct descendant of John Jackson of Wantagh.

★ Elias Hicks married Jemima Seaman in 1771 and moved to Jericho. He was instrumental in the manumission of slaves owned by the members of the Westbury Friends Meeting.

★ Henry Highland Garnet did later attend the African Free School in New York City from 1826-28, come to Jericho and later live in Smithtown with Epenetus Smith, and eventually become a well-known clergyman and abolitionist. He was invited by President Lincoln to visit the White House and speak out about the issues of slavery.

★ The New York State Legislature passed laws in 1799 and 1817 that would provide for the abolition of slavery in New York State. This was a gradual emancipation act. It said that all slaves in New York would be free as of July 4, 1827, ten years after the 1817 bill became law. That was fifty years after the country's first celebration of July 4th.

★ The Fugitive Slave Act, enacted by Congress in 1850, overrode New York State law and made it a criminal offense to assist escaping slaves, with up to six-month imprisonment and a $1,000 fine, and a lucrative reward for slave-catchers. Escaping slaves had long sought refuge in Canada, where England had outlawed slavery in 1833.

★ Members of the Society of Friends, known as Quakers, did help escaping slaves travel by wagon to Long Island, 1830-50, and beyond.

★ "The Old Place" was owned by the Seaman-Hicks families and is a documented stop on the Underground Railroad. The house is still standing on Post Road north of Jericho Turnpike in Old Westbury, New York. It was thought to have been built in 1695, but research is needed to confirm this date vs the later one of 1715.

★ The Maine Maid Inn's secret staircase still exists in the restaurant today—a legacy from its years as Valentine Hicks's house.

★ The verse on Anna's "1850 sampler" is actually derived from the 1855 book *Leaves of Grass* by Walt Whitman. As a young schoolboy in Brooklyn, Walt Whitman listened to the preacher Elias Hicks and is known to have been impressed by what he heard.

★ Henry Hicks of the Hicks Nursery in Westbury did speak as noted in 1941.

An observation about language is important here. The terms "slaves," "colored people," "escaping slaves," and "Negroes" are used in the book because they were used in the years in which the story takes place. Likewise, the term Mulatto used in the 1763 *New-York Gazette* article. Later and today, however, these terms are replaced by language deemed more respectful to this important story—such as enslaved people, Blacks, African Americans, and people of color. The quotations from escaped slave and famed abolitionist Frederick Douglass (page 93) eloquently convey the hardships of slave life in the 1830s, and the great pride in his involvement in the Underground Railroad.

So I here confirm that the most important parts of the story of Brother Jackson and Anna Willis are true, as documented in newspapers, photographs, and other records of the day. The true story of the Underground Railroad in Jericho and Westbury—with each of its stories of people helping people—is an important one in the lives of us all.

Incidentally, my husband and I did years ago find an old suitcase tucked away in the attic of our 1890s house (but not with those fascinating Notebooks and letters!). Fox was my own family's rambunctious collie in 1953, and my brother and sisters and I did live on a street much like Anna's not far from my friend named Brother and the Spry family's farm. And my Father, Matthew W. Gaffney, whom I love dearly, did in fact bring home a goat one year and a lamb another for us to care for and love. The response to this story, in all its stages, by my students from Old Westbury, has encouraged me to write this book, to share our new understandings of a time many generations ago.

The Underground Railroad . . . Village by Village

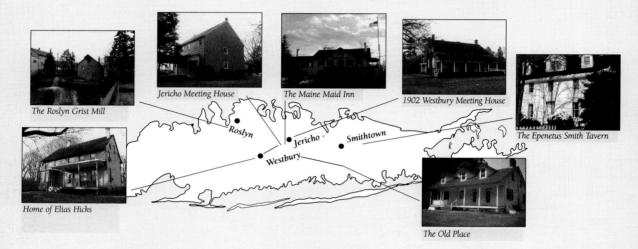

The Roslyn Grist Mill

Jericho Meeting House

The Maine Maid Inn

1902 Westbury Meeting House

The Epenetus Smith Tavern

Home of Elias Hicks

The Old Place

Roslyn • Jericho • Smithtown

Westbury •

"The Underground Railroad . . . Village by Village" describes places and people in Jericho, Port Washington, Roslyn, Smithtown, Wantagh, and Westbury actively involved in the Underground Railroad, 1830-1850 (detail of brochure published by SUNY Old Westbury in 2005; photographs, John Butler; graphics, Leslie Knipe).

"Plantation owners clamored for the return of their property, some coming to New York from far down South to make a search. The Continental Army helped masters recapture people from behind British lines, and King remembered these kidnappings, which could take place without warning:

> *[W]e saw our old masters coming from Virginia, North-carolina, and other parts, and seizing upon their slaves in the streets of New-York, or even dragging them out of their beds. Many of the slaves had very cruel masters, so that the thoughts of returning home with them embittered life to us. For some days we lost our appetite for food, and sleep departed from our eyes."*

- Edward Ball, *Slaves in the Family* (Ballantine Books, New York, 1998) quoting the 1798 memoir of former slave Boston King

---

In the Words of Frederick Douglass

Famed abolitionist and author Frederick Douglass—born a slave in 1817—never knew his father, was separated early from his mother, and was taught to read by the caring wife of a slave master in Baltimore. He escaped to freedom in 1838, and wrote his autobiography in 1845 and enlarged it in 1881. In 1845, lest he be recaptured as a fugitive slave, he went to England—where slavery had been outlawed since 1833. He returned to this country in 1847 after English friends had together bought his freedom, and founded an anti-slavery newspaper called the North Star. *During the Civil War he sought to persuade Abraham Lincoln that former slaves be permitted to join the Union Army.*

Today the writings of Frederick Douglass are admired as eloquent testimony both to the extraordinary hardships endured by slaves and escaping slaves, and to his deep personal reward through participation in the Underground Railroad in Rochester, New York. He stayed in Joseph Post's House in Westbury in 1849, and of this stay wrote to Amy Kirby Post in Rochester, "Here I am seated in the quiet so pleasantly after ten days of confusion in the city. . . . This is a beautiful place." The letter today is part of the collection of Post Family Papers in the Rush Rhees Library, at the University of Rochester.

★

The children unable to work in the field had neither shoes, stockings, jackets, nor trousers, given to them; their clothing consisted of two coarse linen shirts per year. . . . There were no beds given the slaves, unless one coarse blanket be considered such.

★

We were worked in all weathers. It was never too hot or too cold; it could never rain, blow, hail, or snow, too hard for us to work in the field. The longest days were too short for [the overseer], and the shortest nights too long for him. I was somewhat unmanageable when I first went there, but a few months of this discipline tamed me. . . . I was broken in body, soul, and spirit.

★

After my arrival at New York [after escape in 1838], I said I felt like one who had escaped a den of hungry lions. This state of mind, however, very soon subsided; and I was again seized with a feeling of great insecurity and loneliness. I was yet liable to be taken back, and subject to all the tortures of slavery.

★

Thank heaven, I remained but a short time in this distressed situation. I was relieved from it by the humane hand of Mr. David Ruggles, whose vigilance, kindness, and perseverance, I shall never forget. . . . I thought of going to Canada; but he decided against it, in favor of my going to New Bedford, thinking I should be able to get work there at my trade [as a caulker].

★

One important branch of my anti-slavery work in Rochester, was as station master and conductor of the underground railroad passing through this goodly city. Secrecy and concealment were necessary conditions to the successful operation of this rail-road, and hence its prefix "underground." My agency was all the more exciting and interesting, because not altogether free from danger. I could take no step in it without exposing myself to fine and imprisonment, for these were the penalties imposed by the fugitive slave law, for feeding, harboring, or otherwise assisting a slave to escape from his master; but in face of this fact, I can say, I never did more congenial, attractive, fascinating, and satisfactory work. . . . True as a means of destroying slavery, it was like an attempt to bail out the ocean with a teaspoon, but the thought that there was one less slave, and one more freeman, . . . brought to my heart unspeakable joy. On one occasion I had eleven fugitives at the same time under my roof.

Frederick Douglass, Autobiographies, 1845, 1881

Bibliography

Barbour, Hugh, Ed. *Quaker Crosscurrents: Three Hundred Years of Friends of The New York Meetings.* Syracuse, NY: Syracuse University Press, 1995.

Cornell, Thomas C. *Anne and Adam Mott: Their Ancestors and Their Descendants.* Poughkeepsie, NY: A.V. Height, 1890.

Day, Lynda R. *Making a Way to Freedom: A History of African Americans on Long Island.* Interlaken, NY: Empire State Books/Long Island Studies Institute, 1997.

"Friends in the Spirit: African Americans and the Challenge to Quaker Liberalism, 1776-1915." *Long Island Historical Journal* 10 (Fall 1997): 1-15.

Douglass, Frederick. *Narrative of the Life of Frederick Douglass: An American Slave.* Cambridge: Belknap Press of Harvard University, 1960. Several earlier and revised editions of the autobiography exist, published by the author.

Driscoll, James, Derek M. Gray, Richard J. Hourahan and Kathleen G. Velsor. *Angels of Deliverance: The Underground Railroad in Queens, Long Island, and Beyond,* Ed. Wini Warren. Flushing, NY: Queens Historical Society, 1999.

Forbush, Bliss. *Elias Hicks, Quaker Liberal.* New York: Columbia University Press, 1956.

Forbush, William. *Wantagh, Jerusalem and Ridgewood, 1644-1892.* Jamaica, NY: Farmer Printers, 1892.

Gaines, Edith. *The Charity Society, 1794-1994: An Institution for the Use and Benefit of the Poor Among Black People of Jericho.* New York: The Charity Society of Jericho and Westbury Monthly Meetings, 1994.

Hart, Edward, et al. "Flushing Remonstrance," reprint of the 1657 petition. Flushing, NY: The Coalition for Planned Flushing Incorporated, 1993.

Hicks, Henry. "Freeing of Slaves on Long Island by Members of the Religious Society of Friends or Quakers and Self Help Organization Among Colored People." (Speech at celebration of 77th Anniversary of Freeing of the Slaves Organization; and 100th Anniversary of Westbury Fire Company, Westbury, New York, January 9, 1941.) Typescript in archive of the Historical Society of the Westburys, Westbury Public Library.

continued

Jacobs, Harriet A. "Letters from a Slave Girl," Ed. Maria Child, in *Incidents in the Life of a Slave Girl*, Jean Fagan Yellin (Ed.). Cambridge, MA: Harvard University Press, 1987.

Jackson, Mary, letter to Hanna Post, 1823. Post Family Papers, Rush Rhees Library, University of Rochester, Rochester, NY.

Lowery, Ann Gidley. *The Story of Flushing Meeting House*. The Flushing Monthly Meeting of the Religious Society of Friends. New York: Bowne, 1994.

Marcus, Grania Bolton. *A Forgotten People: Discovering the Black Experience in Suffolk County, 1988*. Reprinted under title *Discovering the African-American Experience in Suffolk Country, 1620-1860*. Setauket: Society for the Preservation of Long Island Antiquities, 1995.

Martin, Sister Mary (Mass) R.S.M. *The Hicks Family as Quakers, Farmers and Entrepreneurs*. Ph.D. Dissertation, St. John's University, 1976.

McKernan, Gordon and Allen T. Peppe. *Wantagh Past and Present*. Wantagh, NY: Wantagh School District, 1966. Housed in the Wantagh Public Library.

Naylor, Natalie A., Ed. *Exploring African-American History: Long Island and Beyond*. Hempstead: Hofstra University, Long Island Studies Institute, 1991 (Designed for Teachers).

Onderdonk, Henry Jr. *Annals of Hempstead, 1643-1832;* also "The Rise and Growth of the Society of Friends on Long Island and New York 1657 to 1826." Hempstead, NY: Lott Van de Water, 1878.

Pierce, Jonathan Carpenter. "Letter," August 4, 1939. Housed in Haviland Records, Swarthmore College Library, Swarthmore, PA.

Powell, Aaron M. *Personal Reminiscences of The Anti-Slavery and Other Reforms and Reformers*. New York: Colored Press, 1899.

Powell, Fred J. Family Records and Personal Reminiscences (unpublished manuscript), on loan to Queens Historical Society from Nina Powell.

Robbins, Oscar Burton. "History of the Jackson Family of Hempstead, Long Island, New York, Ohio and Indiana." Unpublished manuscript, 1951. Copy in the Wantagh Public Library.

Schor, Joel. *Henry Highland Garnet: A Voice of Black Radicalism in the Nineteenth Century*. Westport, CT: Greenwood Press, 1977.

Vahey, Mary Feeney. *A Hidden History: Slavery, Abolition, and the Underground Railroad in Cow Neck and on Long Island*. Port Washington: Cow Harbor Peninsula Historical Society, 1998.

Wilson, Warren A. M. "Quaker Hill Sociological Study." Ph.D. Dissertation, Columbia University, 1907.

Willis, Mary Kirby, letter to Isaac Post of Rochester, NY, 1838. Post Family Papers, Rush Rhees Library, University of Rochester, Rochester, NY.

Winsche, Richard A. "Historic Buildings Evaluation," Nassau County Museum Collection, Long Island Studies Institute at Hofstra University.

No Author Listed

"A Short History of Mathias Episcopal Church," unpublished. Vertical File, Wantagh Public Library.

"Inter-departmental Memo: Town of Hempstead, Department of Real Estate, July 10, 1975, Section 56, Block H-8, Lot 52," Jackson File, Wantagh Public Library.

Manumission Society Minutes, New York Historical Society, Roll 1.

"Property Deed." Jackson Vertical File, Wantagh Public Library.

Records of the Committee for Sufferings of the North Carolina Yearly Meeting, letter from Samuel Parsons, 1831. Quaker Reading Room, Guilford College Library, Greensboro, NC.

Interviews

Jean Renison, Westbury Historian. Personal Interviews, 1996, 1997, 1998, 1999.

Leon Rushmore, Member of the Westbury Friends Meeting. Personal Interviews, 2000, 2001.

Maps

Map 14, "Jericho, Syosset, Norwich, Oyster Bay." Baker, Topographical Maps of Kings, Queens Counties of New York. H. S. Walling, New York, 1859.

1890 Map of Nassau County, Long Island Sound, and Westchester County. Thomas C. Cornell, *Anne and Adam Mott: Their Ancestors and Their Descendents.* Poughkeepsie, NY: A.V. Height, 1890.

About the Author
& The Underground Railroad
Teaching Partnership

Kathleen Velsor was born in Rochester, New York. As a young child she lived in nearby LeRoy, New York—an upstate stopping point on the Underground Railroad—and remembers hearing local stories about fugitive slaves. She earned an undergraduate degree in Fine Arts from Lindenwood University in St. Charles, Missouri, and received her Master's degree in Education Administration from Lehigh University in Pennsylvania and her Doctorate in Education and Research from The University of Cincinnati in Ohio.

Dr. Velsor is currently an Associate Professor in the School of Education at the State University of New York at Old Westbury. She has received numerous grants to research the Quaker involvement in the Underground Railroad on Long Island, most recent among them an education grant from the Long Island Community Foundation to establish the Underground Railroad Teaching Partnership to build community through interdisciplinary social studies workshops for school teachers.

The Partnership began its work early in 2005 – to reach out, to tell the story of African-American history on Long Island, bringing together different groups as they examine their own histories. To this end Dr. Velsor lectures frequently to libraries, community groups, and college students as well as to fourth-graders for their local history curriculums, and to middle- and high-school classes. Membership in this small and focused team comprises teachers and other education professionals, with special recognition for the vision of colleague Karon Williams.

In her research supporting the Underground Railroad Teaching Partnership, Dr. Velsor has uncovered a rich history of anti-slavery activity on Long Island that started at least two decades before 1775, the year that the Quakers from Westbury began to free their slaves. This research has been published in three books—*Angels of Deliverance, The Underground Railroad, Queens, Long Island, and Beyond* (1999); *The Road to Freedom, The Underground Railroad, New York and Beyond* (2001); and *Friends of Freedom—The Underground Railroad, Queens, Long Island, and Beyond* (2005)—all published by the Queens Historical Society. In spring 2004 her article "The Long Island Freedom Trail" was published in the *Afro-American Historical and Genealogical Society Journal*, vol. 32.

Kathleen Velsor lives in Bayville, New York, with her family.